Bell, Book, and Scandal

BEDKNOBS AND BROOMSTICKS 3

VELLICHOR BOOKS

An imprint of JustJoshin Publishing, Inc.

Black Cats.
Black Arts.
Black. Mail.

*Must a witch break one set of vows
to keep another?*

Cosmo Saville has never been happier.
His adored police commissioner husband has
finally—mostly— accepted his witchy ways.
And in return, Cosmo has promised to stay out
of police business. It seems their Happily Ever
After has come at last, until Cos discovers John's
sister might be a pawn in a dangerous game of
blackmail…

Commissioner Galbraith is relieved the lies and
secrets are over and his marriage is back on
track. Especially since he has his hands full with
a high-profile suicide and rumors of a citywide
extortion ring. So when John realizes his own
slightly wicked witch is using magic to play
sleuth, all his old fears and doubts return
to haunt him.

With the commissioner's badge and family in
jeopardy, Cosmo feels he has no choice but to
use every power in…his power. Even if that dark
decision costs him everything he cares about most.

BELL, BOOK, AND SCANDAL

Bedknobs and Broomsticks 3

June 2021
Copyright 2021 by Josh Lanyon

Cover by Reese Dante reesedante.com
Cover content is for illustrative purposes only. Any person depicted on the cover is a model.
Editing by Keren Reed
Book design by Kevin Burton Smith

ISBN: 978-1-945802-98-0

Published in the United States of America
JustJoshin Publishing, Inc.
3053 Rancho Vista Blvd.
Suite 116
Palmdale, CA 93551
www.joshlanyon.com

This is a work of fiction. Any resemblance to persons living or dead is entirely coincidental.

To Nicole and Dawn. You know who you are—and where the magic hides.

By the pricking of my thumbs,
Something wicked this way comes.

William Shakespeare, *Macbeth*

Chapter One

"*Merde.*"

I scowled and sucked on the slice across the pad of my thumb. I didn't taste blood, the papercut wasn't that deep, but my tongue tingled with the flavor of...

Odd.

I picked up the letter opener, slit open the envelope, and several glossy black-and-white photos spilled out and slid across my desk.

Black and white? Who took black-and-white photos these days? Who took photos these days? That's what phones were for, right?

I reached for the nearest photograph, studied it curiously—and dropped it as though it had burned my fingertips.

A man and woman locked in naked—very naked—embrace.

I didn't recognize the man, though the large tattooed pentacle on his back indicated maybe I should.

The woman was my sister-in-law. Jinx.

I drew in a deep breath.

Well, this was...unexpected. And unwelcome.

I bowed the envelope to check for a letter. I was anticipating something with misshapen letters cut from magazines and spelling trouble, but there was nothing. Just the photos.

Not that that wasn't plenty right there.

I rested my fingertips on the photos, closed my eyes, concentrated… To my surprise, there it was. The scintilla of the arcane. Magic.

I opened my eyes.

Curiouser and curiouser.

Was there any possibility this wasn't a threat? That the intent was…what? *Hey, here's something you might want to keep an eye on?* I considered that theory hopefully, but I couldn't quite convince myself that these photos had been sent with anything but ill intention.

To what end, though?

Money, right? That was the way these things usually worked. Not that I had any practical experience of blackmail.

Yes. Blackmail.

It wasn't a complete surprise.

Or rather, yes, it was a surprise—especially given that Jinx seemed to be the target—but we weren't the first family in San Francisco to get one of these poison parcels. John had been losing sleep—a lot of sleep—over the past month with the discovery that the city's high society appeared to have fallen prey to a well-connected extortion ring.

John is John Galbraith. My husband—but more importantly, in this context at least, SFPD's new police commissioner.

The plot had only come to light because one of the victims, the Rev. Canon Angela Tzeng had had the guts to go to the police and report an attempt to blackmail her. Tzeng was supposed to be consecrated October 1st as the first female bishop of the Episcopal Diocese of Northern California, but her courageous move had been rewarded by the blackmailer releasing information about a teenaged pregnancy to the press. It was the Twenty-First Century. You'd think— But you'd be wrong. The revelation of Tzeng's youthful mistake was damning information in the eyes of both the public and the diocese. Now Tzeng's very future in the church was in question.

Needless to say, no other victims had come forward. Not openly. Not officially. But they were out there.

"Someone's going to get killed," John had said the other night. He was not a guy for kidding around, and he was not kidding then.

I considered the pile of photos before me. I couldn't help thinking that choosing Jinx as a blackmail target was kind of a stretch.

Yes, these photos were revealing and embarrassing, but at twenty-five, Jinx was a grown woman. The fact that she was a sexually active grown woman would likely only come as a shock to John. She did not hold public office. She was not married. There was no reason I could see that she shouldn't have sex with whoever she pleased, although I had to wonder about her good sense in choosing a guy who'd branded himself with the Sigil of Baphomet.

Jinx had been studying with the Duchess for the past few weeks, so she surely knew better. And if this guy was not a poser, if he was Craft, he ought to know better too. But this photo might be months old. When I'd first met Jinx, she'd been a little bit of an occult fangirl. Actually, she was still a little bit of an occult fangirl.

But I digress. As usual.

That the photos had come to me, made me wonder if Jinx had already been approached and had brushed it off. You have to care a lot about what other people think to make a good blackmail victim. When it came to what other people thought, Jinx had, in the mortal vernacular, zero fucks to give. In fact, there had been a time, and not so long ago, when I thought she'd have taken delight in appalling both John, who was twenty years her senior, and her mother, Nola.

And when it came to Nola, who could blame her? I felt the urge to appall Nola now and then myself. Not that I had to try. My existence was enough to keep my mother-in-law in a constant state of pall.

Which meant what?

That the real target was me? The assumption being that I would pay up to keep Jinx's past from embarrassing her? From embarrassing me? No. From embarrassing *John*.

Of course.

Because John was the vulnerable one. As Police Commissioner, San Francisco's first gay police commissioner at that, John was the one with something to lose. The news that the police commissioner's younger sister was a devil worshipper (oh, I could already hear all the idiotic and ignorant things people would say) would certainly bother the hell out of John—and might even impact his political future. John was an ambitious man. A man with a plan.

So why not send this packet to John?

Oh, right. Because John was as honorable as he was ambitious. He would not be blackmailed. He would see Jinx burned alive—in the court of public opinion, that is—before he paid one cent of blackmail money.

The blackmailer was relying on me to pay up to protect John from himself.

Mistake.

If I had learned anything in the four months I'd been married to John, it was that honesty was the best policy. At least with John.

When I stepped out of the office, I found Blanche, my assistant, struggling valiantly to load a seventeenth century Nuremberg wrought-iron pirate chest onto a hand truck.

Blanche is a curvaceous fifty-something. She's an expert on eighteenth century jewelry, makes the best vegan cheesecake this side of Sacramento, and favors Elvira Mistress of the Dark eye makeup. She is also Wicca, a loyal friend, and a great employee. What she is *not*, is a deckhand or a longshoreman. I rushed to her aid.

"What the—? Blanche, you're going to throw your back out."

She gasped out, "No worries," but hastily moved out of my way.

I managed to redirect the chest's landing so it did not topple over the tall and very narrow Italian Regency apothecary chest. Blanche leapt to save the gilt and violet SF & Co. water basin and pitcher rocking precariously on the nearby dining table.

"*No worries?* This thing's nearly two hundred pounds." I managed to shimmy the loading platform beneath the bottom of the trunk and leveraged it a few inches off the floor. Awkwardly, I maneuvered my unwieldly cargo through the obstacle course posed by plush carpet and fragile furniture to its new home by the large bay windows at the front of Blue Moon Antiques' showroom. I lowered it to the floor with a little *oof* of relief.

"It *is* heavier than it looks," Blanche admitted.

I glanced around the long, furniture-crowded space. Sunlight gilded old wood and fragile porcelain, glittered off a decorative string of benignly smiling jack-o'-lantern faces.

"Where's Ambrose? I asked him to move this thing."

Blanche murmured something vague, and I glanced at her. Behind heart-shaped rhinestone spectacles, her blue-green gaze was evasive.

"What?"

"Oh. Well… He had to leave."

I frowned. "Had to leave why?"

"I'm not exactly sure. Something to do with his grandmother."

"Not again!"

She raised her hands in a now-don't-get-excited gesture. "I think it really was an emergency."

"It's *always* an emergency."

Blanche didn't bother to argue because it was true.

"This can't go on. The whole point in hiring him was because we need someone *here*."

"I know." Blanche sounded sympathetic. As though Ambrose's irresponsible behavior didn't affect her too.

"I mean, I like him. I think he's a good kid. He's a big help when he's here. But he's never here."

"Yes. True." Her expression was regretful.

I brooded for a moment or two. "Okay. Don't worry. I'll deal with it."

Behind the sparkling red glasses, Blanche's eyes went wide with alarm. "Cos, you're not— Are you going to fire him?"

I hesitated. "I'm not sure. Probably not? Not today. Not without talking to him. But this *can't* go on."

"I know. I know." Her tone was soothing.

"I know you know."

"It's just he's in such a difficult situation."

I nodded. This was so. Ambrose was sole caretaker of his elderly grandmother.

She added persuasively, "And he *is* trained now."

"Whatever that means."

Blanche said coaxingly, "He's used to us? We're used to him?"

I opened my mouth. Closed it. Shook my head.

* * * * *

I arrived at City Hall one minute after noon. Pat Anderson, John's charming and ruthlessly efficient executive assistant, apologetically informed me that John's meeting with "The Brass" had gone into overtime.

In this case "The Brass" meant Mayor Stevens, Police Chief Morrisey, Deputy Chief Danville, the Board of Supervisors, various elected officers, and other entities.

"Uh-oh," I said. "That sounds like a recipe for indigestion."

"I wish I'd known you had a lunch date, Mr. Saville. I could have—"

"No, no. This was spur-of-the-moment."

"Ah." Pat's smile was sympathetic—I was getting that a lot today.

I was trying to think if there was a way I could slip in for a quick word with John. This wasn't an emergency, exactly, but the situation was certainly urgent. John would certainly think it was urgent.

"I'm so sorry your vacation plans had to be canceled," Pat was saying.

"Hm? Yes. Thanks." John and I had been planning to travel back to Salem, Massachusetts to visit my father for the holiday, but then Reverend Tzeng had shown up on SFPD's doorstep with her tale of harassment and extortion. "Business before pleasure. Pat, do you think there's any chance—"

Pat was opening her mouth to regretfully inform me there was no chance in hell, when the door to the conference room flew open and a crowd of grim-faced men and women in business attire streamed out, all of them talking at once as they answered their phones, checked for text messages, and nodded distractedly to each other.

John was at the back of the crowd, handsome and imposing in a dark gray suit with micro checks. That is, *I* think he's handsome, but his features are too severe, too fierce to ever sell anything but truth, justice, and the American Way. Like the others, he was grim-faced, so I deduced the meeting had not gone well for anyone. My heart squeezed at the uncharacteristic weariness I saw in his face. I hated to think I was about to add to his already considerable stress.

He didn't see me at first. He was talking with Sergeant Pete Bergamasco, his bodyguard and general factotum. Bergamasco is one of those brusque former military types, but beneath his olive drab exterior beats a heart that burns with devotion for John. Not romantically. Bergamasco is not gay.

Even if he were gay, I'm pretty sure he wouldn't be the romantic type. But he is definitely a one-man dog. He tolerates me.

"Pat, can you push my one o'clock back to two and my two to tomorrow?" John called over the din of voices.

"On it." Pat reached for the phone.

John was a big guy, the tallest man present, and at last his restless gaze lit on me lurking by the doorway. His face brightened. "Hey," he said, coming to meet me.

"Hi."

He kissed me, and we got some smiles from the others as they filed past. Technically, we were still newlyweds, and most people have a soft spot for the newly married. Not including Sergeant Bergamasco.

"Cos. Were you hoping for lunch? I can't get away today."

"Another day would be lovely. Can I talk to you?"

John hesitated, glanced at the line of lawmakers funneling out the door into the hallway, glanced at Bergamasco, who looked resigned.

"Just for a minute," I said quickly. "It's important, or I wouldn't ask."

John's amber eyes met mine, and his expression softened. "Of course." He put his hand on my back, guiding me through the queue, which made way as though before Moses parting the Red Sea.

We stepped into John's very large mahogany-paneled corner office. He closed the door, and the thick carpet and thicker walls instantly swallowed the reception area noise in a gulp.

"What's wrong?"

"This came in yesterday's mail. I only opened it this morning." I handed over the manila envelope.

John frowned, took the envelope, peered inside. He drew out a photo. His face changed.

"Jesus Christ."

"Blanche handled it, I handled it, the mail person handled it, so I don't know about fingerprints. But there was a very faint scintilla…"

I stopped talking. He wasn't listening.

I studied his stony face, said, "She's a grown woman, John. She isn't doing anything wrong."

I could see myself come back into focus. John growled, "You don't know that. This guy could be married. This guy could be…anything."

"Anything" meaning *nothing good*, as evidenced by the sigil tattooed on Jinx's unknown partner's back. But this was not about me, not about the Craft, and I did not take offense.

"Okay. Fair enough. But my point is, Jinx's actions don't reflect on you. Don't reflect on your office."

He threw me a look of impatience, but his voice was quiet, even, as he said, "Of course they do, Cos. In the court of public opinion? My sister's actions absolutely reflect on me."

I wanted to argue, but maybe he was right. In fact, he probably *was* right.

He drew out another photo, studied it with hard eyes. "Goddamn it," he said softly. His gaze rose to meet mine. "Did you know about this? Do you know who this is?"

"No," I said quickly. "I had—have—no idea."

For a moment I was afraid the old suspicions and misunderstandings that had nearly torn us apart before would resurface, but he accepted it with a little nod. He turned away, went to his desk, and dumped the photos out. With a couple of quick movements, he arranged them in a large square and then stared down at the big picture.

"Do you think she's in love with him?" He didn't look at me.

"I don't know."

"I hope not."

I went to join him at the desk. He said, "You see how, no matter their position, his face is hidden? That's not coincidence. He's part of this. He set her up."

John was right. Or at least, he was right that in every photo, the face of Jinx's companion was obscured. Personally, I thought the giant sigil carved on the gentleman's back would be kind of a giveaway in a lineup.

Not that having sex with the police commissioner's sister was grounds for arrest or even being thrown into a lineup.

Not so far anyway.

"I see."

"Maybe, just maybe, this time they've slipped up."

"But are you sure this is connected to your extortion case? It could be a co—"

"I'm sure." He sounded sure, no lie.

I considered John's stern profile.

"John…"

He glanced at me. Once again, his face seemed to lose some of its hardness. "What?"

"I think I could be of help." I tried to phrase it carefully because I knew he would be instinctively resistant to my offer. "When I opened the envelope, there was scintilla. Just a trace."

"A trace of…a trace? What?"

"Scintilla. It's hard to explain in words, hard to translate."

"I know what scintilla means."

"No, but in this context—"

His reddish brows drew together. "What context?"

"The context of-of Craft. Of magic."

Instantly, his features grew shuttered, closed. "No."

"You haven't heard me out."

"This doesn't have anything to do with magic. This is extortion. Plain and simple—and all too human."

I said quietly, "I'm human, John."

His whisky-colored eyes widened. "I know that," he said quickly, and put his arms around me, as though sheltering me from his words. "That isn't what I meant. You realize that, right? I understand that you want to help. I appreciate the offer. But no. This is not a time, not a situation for magic. This is police business."

"I understand, yes. But—"

He brushed my hair back from my face. "I don't want you involved. This is an ugly, sordid, god-awful mess, and I don't want you anywhere near it."

I tried to interject, but he was still speaking.

"And you promised you would stay out of police business. Remember? You promised you would try not to use magic."

I *had* promised. I had promised not to use magic as a first resort. In fact, I had sworn to only use magic as a last resort.

I closed my mouth. Swallowed the words he did not want to hear.

"I'm holding you to that promise, Cos." His voice was gentle, but he was dead serious. "I'm touched that you want to help, but I mean it. I don't want you involved. I don't want you to use magic."

I said nothing. My heart was pounding very hard, as though I was facing some terrible threat, but the truth was, this was a promise I had made willingly, had made with all my heart.

John was still gentle, still steely. His eyes saw too much, saw everything. "Do you understand?"

"Yes," I said huskily. "I understand."

Chapter Two

Oakland's earliest inhabitants were the Lisjan Ohlone people. These Huchiun natives lived there for thousands of years, so safe to say, there were *plenty* of posterns in that part of town, and I had no problem landing on Ambrose's doorstep.

Well, not literally his doorstep. More like the landing of the Bancroft Avenue apartment he shared with his grandmother.

I don't know what it was like in prehistoric times, but these days Eastmont is not a great neighborhood. In fact, the violent-crime rate is just about 700% over the national average. But the place looked okay. Bruised and battered but still standing. The blue building was gated and surrounded by autumn-colored trees. It was also surrounded by other apartment buildings and busy streets—and all the ground floor windows had bars across them—but there were definitely worse places.

No sound came from inside the apartment. I knocked softly on the peeling white door—and then knocked again.

I was getting ready to knock a third time when I heard locks turning and door chains sliding. The door swung open, and Ambrose stood in the doorway. A slight, almost frail-looking twenty-one-year-old in ripped jeans and a black sweatshirt. That afternoon his wiry dark hair looked wilder than usual, and he was wide-eyed—not with delight.

"C-Cosmo!"

I said, "Hey. I happened to not be in the neighborhood but decided to swing by anyway."

He gulped. "I— Didn't Blanche tell you I had to—that it was a-an emergency?"

"She told me."

His creamy complexion went ghostly. He raised his chin to meet his fate head on. "Are you here to fire me?"

"I hope not." I was sincere about that. "But we definitely need to talk. May I come in?"

Ambrose threw an uneasy glance over his shoulder, hesitated, but then moved aside. "I guess so. Yes."

I stepped inside. The apartment smelled of candles, thyme, and stewing beef. It took my eyes a second or two to adjust to the gloom. The blinds were closed tightly, and the only light came from a small reading lamp at the end of a sagging sofa. A large book lay open on the coffee table in front of the sofa. Next to the book was a calligraphy pen set and a small indigo bottle of ink.

"GramMa is sleeping," Ambrose whispered. "She had a bad night."

"I'm sorry to hear it."

"Did you…want to sit down?"

"Thank you. I would." I went to the sofa, but the book on the coffee table caught my attention. I stared down at a diagram of the Cygnus constellation, looked up to find him watching me warily.

"You're working on your grimoire?"

He nodded, dark eyes watchful.

Some of my tension eased. In June I had agreed to take Ambrose on as my apprentice in the Craft, which made firing him complicated. It would be difficult to continue as his master if there were hard feelings over his losing his job. Then again, I had started wondering if maybe he needed a different master anyway because we had argued repeatedly over his lack of interest in my training methods—in particular the building of his grimoire. It had turned into such a point of contention that I had refused to teach him another spell until he showed me that he had made some progress on his personal Book of Shadows.

To be honest, he could be so muleheaded, I hadn't expected to win this battle so quickly. Or at all.

"May I see?"

Ambrose nodded again, moving to the table, picking up the book and handing it to me.

I took it carefully. Handling another's grimoire must always be done with respect—and caution. But as I turned the fragile pages, I smiled. He had taken a book on natural history from the 1920s and overlaid several pages of text with his own notes, diagrams, and the spells I'd shared with him. The full-color plates of creatures both real and imaginary remained intact. It was beautifully done.

"Is it all right?" he asked gruffly.

"Oh yes. Very much so." I met his gaze. "Are you happy with it?"

He shrugged, but then smiled reluctantly. "Yeah. You were right. It's kind of in—"

The door to the apartment's sole bedroom opened, and Ambrose broke off.

"Who here?" The voice was small and creaky.

An elderly woman swaddled in sweaters and a flannel nightie shuffled a few steps into the living room. She was tiny, fine-boned, and so pale she looked silver, inexplicably reminding me of a chimaera fish. Her white hair was in a braid that reached her waist. Her eyes were white too, and I remembered she was blind.

Ambrose threw me a quick, nervous look. "It's my boss, GramMa. It's Mr. Saville."

"I'm sorry to intrude, Madame," I said.

She stopped a few feet from us, swaying ever so slightly as though rocked by an unseen current. She began to sniff the air. Which was...a little different.

There was something else a little different about her, and I understood where Ambrose's talent sprang from.

"There dark powa here," she whispered.

My scalp prickled.

"No, GramMa," Ambrose said quickly.

"No, Madame," I said. "I promise you I mean no harm to you or to Ambrose."

"You ave come yah to take my son!"

"No. No, really, I haven't."

Ambrose pleaded, "GramMa, Mr. Saville is my boss. He's my master."

I doubt she even heard him. She pointed at me and began to cast her spell.

Some of the words were French, some English, some... something else. Jamaican Patois perhaps? While words matter in spellcasting, intent matters more, and despite her age and mental confusion, her intent was focused and deadly. As the air began to change, grow misty and green, I made the avert sign. The coffee table flipped over, flinging blue ink everywhere, and the lamp next to the couch exploded.

"No, no! GramMa, no. Please no!" Ambrose was crying. He did not attempt to stop her, of course, would never have dreamed of using Craft against her.

Nor could I. Or rather, I could have, but such an act would be unthinkable.

It would also be unthinkable to let her slay me.

Open the door that hides within
Protect this crone from mortal sin
I shall return another day
But just for now I must away

The door to the apartment flew open at the same moment a blue rectangle appeared. I opted for the rectangle and sprang through the frame of light.

I landed on my hands and knees on a high wooden platform.

A high wooden platform surrounded by yellow prison bars and crowded with small children, one of whom shouted into my face, "It's MY turn!"

"I—right. I see that." I looked around and saw also that, in addition to the munchkins, there were several alarmed-looking women already on their feet and closing in on what turned out to be a large and elaborate play structure, complete with a plastic green palm tree that was preventing me from standing.

This is what comes of relying on kiddie Craft. And relying on kiddie Craft is what comes when you make promises you shouldn't make.

"You're too BIG," another tiny terror bellowed, and kicked me with her pink daisy sneaker.

"Ouch! All *right*. I'm going…"

I dove down the wavy blue plastic slide, arms first, and landed ungracefully in a pile of sand and scattered toys. I could hear the cell phones clicking like paparazzi as I scrambled up and sprinted away, hands raised to shield my face.

* * * * *

"You can stop laughing now," I told Andi.

We were sitting in the back office of the Mad Batter, the specialty cupcake shop Andi owns and operates.

I suppose you could say Andromeda Merriweather is my best friend, but when you've known someone as long as I've known Andi—all my life, in fact—the bond is closer to blood tie than friendship. And I say that as someone raised in a society where blood is everything.

Anyway, Andi is three months older than me. She's tall and lanky, wears her coppery hair short and spiky, has hazel eyes and freckles as cute as cupcake sprinkles. Despite all that refined sugar, she's not a frivolous person, but she laughs easily, and she was still laughing as she pushed a red-brown cream-cheese-topped cupcake my way.

"Sorry. But you have to admit, if this happened to Bree or V. or Whitby…"

"I'd be laughing my ass off if it happened to Whitby," I agreed. Waite Whitby is my first cousin on my mother's side, which means that if I were to break my neck falling off a kiddie play structure, he would take my place in the direct line of succession to *trône de sorcière*.

Well, no, because he'd have to get my mother and *his* mother out of the way first, but anyway, he'd definitely move up a rung on the ladder. Which is something he's been aware of since he was seven and I was five and he tried to drown me in the fountain of our aunt Laure d'Estrées' Parisian garden.

Not that you need to know about that now.

I took a bite of cupcake and raised my eyebrows. "Mmm. What *is* that?"

"Devil in Red Velvet."

"Wow." I savored another lusciously creamy sweet bite, said slowly, thickly, "Did you…?"

"Just a pinch," she admitted.

"Kind of pushing the envelope, don't you think?"

She acknowledged it. "They're not for my regular customers. I'm thinking of starting an exclusive line, catering to Craft clients."

I nodded. The idea bothered me, no lie. There's so much bias against mortals, but I really didn't expect that of Andi. For one thing, she's in love with a mortal—although she won't admit it.

"How's Trace?" I asked, none too subtly. Trace Levine was probably John's best friend. They grew up together, served in the SEALs together, and Trace had been Best Man at our wedding, which was where he'd met Andi.

She made a face, reading me correctly. "He's fine. Everything is great between us."

You would think that would be good news. But you would be wrong. Her sigh was wistful.

I changed the subject. Only not really. "Does John talk much to Trace?" I asked.

"Sure."

"I mean, like we talk."

"Oh." Andi moved her head in negation. "No. John's so busy these days. But no. He doesn't talk to Trace about police business. Or even family business. Not anymore."

I felt a little twinge over that "not anymore" because I knew that was John keeping my secrets.

She slid a blue mini cupcake with green and teal sprinkles my way. "Try this Neptune's Nibble."

I said regretfully, "I think I'm cupcaked out."

"Not possible." She tilted her head, studying me. "What are you going to do about Ambrose?"

At this reminder I checked my phone once again for messages, but there was still no word from Ambrose. I did see a message from my belle-mère, but pretended I didn't.

"I don't know. I certainly have a better understanding of the situation."

She said slowly, "Does John realize you've taken Ambrose as your apprentice? Because you promised not to use magic, but how can you instruct the kid without using any magic of your own?"

"Right now, I'm just teaching him the history of the Abracadantès and a few basic spells. Elementary stuff. The Ten Precepts. How to build a grimoire. That kind of thing."

"But you must be demonstrating the spells first. Anyway, isn't that splitting hairs?"

I sighed my exasperation. It's so annoying when people who disagree with you are right. "Yes. And yes. And no, John doesn't know that I'm training Ambrose in witchcraft."

Her hazel eyes were sympathetic. But she also thought I'd brought this on myself by promising John not to use Craft. And she was right about that too. "Do you think *grand-mère* is dangerous?"

"Hell to the yeah, *grand-mère* is dangerous. If she could have killed me, she would have. I don't know if she poses a threat to mortals, but she sure as heck poses a threat to anyone Craft who crosses her path."

"But that's not likely, right? Surely, she doesn't go out. Does she?"

"I have no idea what she does or doesn't do. For all I know she has a regular gig performing magic tricks at the senior center. I'm ashamed to admit, I didn't give it much thought until now. I figured it was something Ambrose should be able to work out on his own, but this is not easily managed. I'm going to ask the Duchess if she has any ideas."

"Has she ever *not* had an idea?" Andi said dryly.

"True."

Andi licked a glittering sprinkle off her fingertip. "Speaking of your mother, I saw Phelon on Tuesday. He was having dinner at Gary Danko's."

Phelon Penn is one of Maman's Cavalier King Charles Spaniels. I'm sorry. Did I say that aloud? Phelon Penn is my mother's former companion. Like the other Cavalier King Charles Spaniel, he was the perfect lapdog and cost a fortune in grooming supplies.

"Was he alone?"

"No."

"Was he with a woman?"

"Yes."

I smiled and reached for the Neptune's Nibble.

Chapter Three

"Hey! It's John, isn't it?" Our waiter—a dark-haired guy in his thirties with big blue eyes and a boyish grin—beamed in recognition.

John glanced at him, did a double take, glanced at me. "That's right," he said with an un-John-like brightness. "Lance, right? Lance, this is my husband, Cosmo."

Lance also glanced at me. His face didn't exactly fall, but he was clearly disappointed. "Husband?" he repeated. "Gosh. I didn't see *that* coming."

"Oh, are you psychic?" I inquired.

John cleared his throat.

"Hm?" Lance spared me another distracted look—he was having trouble tearing his gaze from John.

I opened my mouth, but John spoke over me in that fake-hearty voice, "But come he did!"

I smiled at him. "Many times," I said. "Many, *many* times."

John turned the color of his beloved Pinot Noir.

"Ohhhhkay, then!" Lance said. "I'll just get that wine list, shall I?" He sprinted away.

"Gosh. I didn't see *that* coming," I said to John.

He laughed, shook his head chidingly. "Lance was a long time ago."

"I should hope."

He reached across the table, lightly traced my ring finger and the platinum Celtic eternity knot wedding band. "I don't remember how many Lances there were, but there's only one you."

I cocked an eyebrow. "Spoken like a true romantic."

It was John's turn to laugh.

Actually, he was a romantic. I didn't realize it at first—and he would have denied it. But so it was. It was one of a number of things I had initially gotten wrong about John. Like assuming he was a snob. That wasn't really fair. John didn't care about price tags or name brands. He simply wanted the best he could afford, whether in ties or wines or swimming pool liners. It wasn't anything to do with compensating for growing up poor or being ambitious or trying to impress people with his worldly goods. John was a pragmatist, pure and simple.

He believed in doing things right the first time. He believed in paying for quality because it eliminated waste, improved efficiency, and cost less in the long run.

That said, he did care about appearances. *Optics.*

Not always. Not above all else. Though Mayor Stevens had pushed hard for my arrest when I had been suspected of murdering Seamus Reitherman, John had not postponed our wedding, let alone—as you might expect—ended our engagement. In fact, I found out later, he had threatened to resign as commissioner if I was arrested.

But he felt it was important to be seen at the right places doing the right things. We attended a lot of high-profile social events out of duty rather than enjoyment, and a couple of nights a week we dined out at expensive restaurants where there was a very good chance our photo would end up in the next day's papers.

Which is what we were doing at Izzy's Steakhouse in the Marina District on Friday night. The original Izzy's had been a Barbary Coast saloon legendary for its thick, juicy steaks and Prohibition hooch. The current incarnation offered a highbrow take on the classic model: dark wood and deep booths, a cozy fireplace and specialty cocktails. At least Izzy's was actually one of John's favorite places, and once we'd got our drinks and meals were ordered, I could see him slowly relaxing under the soothing influence of soft lights, a second glass of wine, and piano jazz.

I relaxed too. It had been a long and fraught day, but sitting here with John put everything into perspective again.

"Have you spoken to Jinx yet?" I asked when I'd finished giving him the abbreviated version of my day's activities.

"No."

That surprised me because John is not one for putting off today what he'd have done three days ago if he'd known about it.

I must have looked my surprise because he said, "We've been getting along okay these last couple of months. I'm not looking forward to blowing it all up."

"Do you have to blow it up? Isn't there a way to talk to her without it turning into a confrontation?"

"No. Not about something like this. Regardless of how I put it, the words I choose, my tone, my expression, she's going to look at this as me challenging her right to live her own life the way she chooses."

He was probably right. Largely because, for most of the time I'd known John, he'd done that very thing to Jinx. Their truce was fragile. And yet, I knew they did love each other.

"You're just asking for a name, right?"

"That would be the starting point," John agreed. Or sort of agreed.

I watched him for a moment. "Why don't I ask her?"

His brows drew into a straight, forbidding line.

I persisted, "After all, the envelope came to me. It was intended for me. That's something she ought to know."

"I wasn't planning to withhold anything," John said.

"That's what I'm afraid of." I was only half teasing. I waited, sipping my *Automne en Normandie* cocktail. According to the drinks menu, a sweetly tart concoction of Laird's apple brandy, Granny Smith apple, honey syrup, and a splash of fresh lemon juice. Strong enough to knock Snow White on her ass, for sure.

He said slowly, almost reluctantly, "You do seem better able to communicate with her."

I laughed. "You make her sound like an alien life form."

"Sometimes I feel like she is." But his smile was rueful.

Our meals arrived on a waft of cracked peppercorn and bay leaf: filet mignon for me and rack of lamb for John. John ordered another bottle of wine.

When the now-subdued Lance departed again, I said tentatively, "If this guy, this friend of Jinx's is Cr—like me—"

"French?" John was still smiling, but there was a glint in his eyes.

I cleared my throat. "Yes. French. I could be of help to your investigation."

I wasn't halfway through my sentence before he was shaking his head. "Cos, the department has its own occult expert."

"I know. Solomon Shimon. But he might not actually be, er, French. Maybe he's *Canadien français*, which shares some commonalities but isn't the same as being *un citoyen français*. If you understand my meaning?"

"*Mais oui.* I get it. All the same, you don't work for SFPD; Shimon does. He's our guy. He's our occult expert; you're married to the police commissioner. Equally important but different roles."

He wasn't trying to be patronizing. He thought I was feeling jealous or competitive with this unknown occult expert.

"I understand. I just want *you* to understand that I'm a-a valuable resource. If you need me. I can guarantee I have connections Shimon won't."

John smiled faintly. "I appreciate that offer."

"I don't think you do, but it's true."

He let that pass, said diplomatically, "You know, you'll be able to evaluate Shimon for yourself tomorrow evening."

A sherry-roasted mushroom fell off my fork. "He's going to be at the Stevenses' Halloween party?"

"So I hear. You might be pleasantly surprised. I hope you will. He's not one of these kooks we see on nightly news human-interest segments."

"You're killing me with the compliments."

John looked like he wasn't sure if I was joking. "He takes this stuff as seriously as you do. That's all I'm getting at. He's got an impressive clearance rate—"

My cell phone buzzed into life, and the whole table jittered with it, knocking silverware against plates, nearly overturning the wineglasses.

"Jesus," John said, grabbing for the wine bottle before it spilled.

"Sorry."

Technology is not my friend. I've had one television, three microwaves, and five cell phones blow up at my touch—and still counting.

I looked down and recognized, with relief, Ambrose's owl symbol. "It's Ambrose. Excuse me. I have to take this."

John muttered something, hastily mopping at the contents of the spilled wineglasses.

I threaded my way through the crowded tables and stepped outside. The evening air was cool and scented of the marina and woodsmoke. Overhead, the painted sign of Izzy Gomez creaked in the October breeze.

"Hey. Everything okay?" I asked.

"I'm so sorry, Cos." Ambrose's voice was high and shaky. "She never did that before."

"It's okay. Are you okay? Is she okay?" I was beginning to sound like a self-help guru for witches.

"Me? I'm fine. Cos, I'm so, *so* s—"

"Not your fault. Not hers either. Why didn't you tell me things had gotten this bad? I didn't realize what you were dealing with."

"What could you do about it?"

"I don't know. But maybe together we can figure something out."

Ambrose still sounded very young, very wobbly as he tried to explain. "She was always in two minds about her power, you know? She was raised in the church, and so she always thought maybe this was wrong. It's why she wouldn't ever really teach me any spells."

"I see." I was starting to. "Are you coming in to the shop tomorrow?"

"I can't. Not until Monday. Not until the lady next door is back. Usually, she watches her during the day, but she's been visiting family this week and GramMa kept getting out of the apartment."

The picture his words painted was truly disturbing. Was he tying her to the bed? Locking her in a closet?

"Okay. Got it. Then I'll see you on Monday and we'll start figuring out what we can do to make life a little easier for you and your *grand-mère*."

He burst out, "Why would you? I nearly got you *killed*." His voice cracked on "killed."

I made a dismissive sound—alarmingly reminiscent of my mother. "*Quelle absurdité!* You didn't invite me over. That was my own idea. And not to be immodest, but I think I can take your grandma in hand-to-hand."

Ambrose gave a weak laugh. I could only imagine what the last few hours had been like for him. Had he been chasing the old girl all through the city as she jumped from postern to postern? It was very possible.

"Try not to worry," I said.

I was worried enough for both of us.

"Did you want me to contact social services?" John asked on the drive home to Greenwich Street. "See if I can pull some strings?"

This is one of the things I love about John. When he offers help, it isn't just lip service. He will try to come up with real and practical solutions. Sometimes whether you want them or not.

"I'd have to ask Ambrose. There may be certain…complications." Like my understanding that the old lady subsisted on social-security fraud. I wasn't going to share that possibility with John, though.

"I hope the kid isn't not asking for assistance out of misguided pride. This is why we have local government," John said. "To provide a safety net."

He was holding my hand, and I squeezed him back in a silent thank-you. Aloha's eyes met mine in the rearview mirror. She smiled faintly.

The city provided John with a car and an official driver by the name of Aloha Newman. Aloha was a short, stocky woman of about thirty. She was a Hawaiian transplant. I suspected she was perhaps descended from the Menehune, but had never seen any indication of supernatural ability—beyond being always able to find a parking space, no matter how crowded the city.

The limo turned down the long narrow drive leading to our cul-de-sac. Coit Tower glimmered in the distance. Lights shone cheerfully in the townhouses across from ours, illuminating paper ghosts and sparkly jack-o'-lanterns in windows— Halloween was only a week away. The building next to us was still dark, still uninhabited. The property manager had been forced to file for bankruptcy.

Aloha pulled in front of 1132, and John and I piled out before she could unbuckle her seat belt.

"Commish!" she objected, as she always did.

"We're good," John told her.

She shook her head. "Do you need me tomorrow night, Commissioner?"

"No. I'll drive us to the mayor's party. See you Monday. Have a good weekend."

"Same bat time, same bat channel!"

John shoved the door shut, and the limo silently rolled away, its red taillights climbing skyward until they vanished over the crest of the drive.

"That was a long-ass day." John put his arm around me as we walked up the steps to our townhouse. I sighed agreement.

Pyewacket, the three-hundred-year-old Familiar who inhabits the body of a Russian Blue cat, greeted us inside the enclosed loggia. I picked him up, bumped my face against his furry one. "Hello, you."

Pye purred hello.

"What's he doing loose?" John unlocked our front door.

I murmured, "He loves the nightlife. He got to boogie on the disco 'round, oh yea," and Pye meowed in accompaniment—and then conveyed the real news of the evening.

"Are you *kidding*? John—"

John had already pushed open the door, stepped inside, and turned on the light. The night breeze gusting through the living room from the wide-open French doors leading onto the back patio slammed the door shut again, cutting us off.

I yanked it open. "John!"

John swung back to me, his expression hard and dangerous. He put a hand on my shoulder and pushed me back a couple of steps. "Stay outside. We've had a break-in."

I planted my hand on the door, which he was trying to close in my face. "I know. It's okay. They're gone now."

John stopped trying to propel me out of harm's way. "What do you mean they're gone?"

"Pye says they're gone."

"*Pye* says?"

It's not like we hadn't been through this. But I think even after four-plus months, it was hard for John to accept that Pyewacket was more than a surly cat with a taste for Friskies Paté and Jewel of Russia Ultra Black Label.

"Pye was here when they…broke in." I faltered because they had not *broken* in, they had used an unlocking spell. Our intruders were definitely Craft. That, in my opinion, was the worst news of the night.

John made a sound of exasperation. "If you and the Cat on the Mat don't mind, I'm going to check for myself." He closed the door firmly and, to my irritation, locked it.

Still cradling Pyewacket, I put my hand up and snapped my fingers. You don't need an unlocking spell for your own front door. The deadbolt turned, and the door swung open.

John was already halfway up the staircase leading to the master bedroom, the second guest bedroom, and his office. Oh, and the gun safe. He glanced back, but apparently decided to choose his battles, because he continued upstairs without a word.

I looked around the front room. Other than the open French doors, everything seemed normal. Well, I mean there was a skeleton sprawled facedown on the hardwood floor, and several vintage black sequin-covered cat pop-ups lay on the coffee table, but that was from me not finishing putting up the Halloween decorations.

"What were they looking for?" I asked Pyewacket. "Do you know?"

Pye did not know. He had not stuck around long enough to find out.

"Who were they? Do I know them?"

The best Pye could do there was assure me *he* did not know them. He jumped from my arms and disappeared up the staircase after John.

I closed my eyes, attempting a *Sort de découverte*. It's a very old spell, and, in these days of electronic surveillance, nearly obsolete.

Quem oportet te habere altitudo, pondus, et aetatis,
et sexus, ubi es?
Tu quis es, mille rerum, sed quisque elegit artifex

videre quæ vos decies non quod tibi nomen est?
Ex quo non sis et sis mihi.
Ostende faciem tuam!

I think there were problems with my recollection of the spell, but in any case, before I finished speaking, John came back down the stairs, and I broke off.

If John had noticed me waving my arms and chanting Latin in our living room, he didn't mention it.

"They broke into my desk. It doesn't seem like they took anything. They were in your office as well. You'll want to take a look, but I'm guessing you won't find anything missing."

"If they weren't here to rob us, why…" I tailed off at John's expression.

John said bleakly, "My guess? They were looking for something they could use to blackmail us with."

Chapter Four

The police came and went.

The fact that the police commissioner's own home had been broken into meant the case would be given highest priority. The fact that nothing had been removed from the police commissioner's home meant the case would be downgraded to lowest of high priority in a city where there are over fifty thousand property crimes a year.

Disconcertingly—for John and the boys and girls in blue—no one showed up on the footage of our surveillance cameras. Our security system showed no signs of having been disarmed, and yet had not been triggered by the intruders.

After the uniformed officers had reluctantly, apologetically retreated, John poured us each a glass of wine, and we settled on the sectional sofa in the sunken living room.

It was nearly midnight by then. We toasted a little wearily.

"*¡Arriba.*" John touched the rim of his glass to mine.

"*Abajo.*"

"*Al centro.*" We clicked the bowls.

"*Adentro.*" We drank. I finished, "Abracadabra."

John expelled an amused breath, leaned forward, and kissed me. I kissed him back. Our mouths lingered, but then he drew back—reluctantly, at least—and said, "Do you have an explanation for what happened here tonight?"

"I think you called it. I think someone was looking for information that could be used against us."

"That's not what I mean, though."

I made a face. "I know. But you're not going to like hearing what I believe happened."

"Hearing things I don't like is part of my job description."

I sighed, let my head fall back on his outstretched arm. "I think magic was used to break in here tonight. I think that's why no one showed up on the surveillance tapes. I think that's why the alarm wasn't triggered."

"Magic." His tone was flat.

"You asked. That's what I believe."

He groaned softly, tipped his head back to stare at the ceiling. "I really have a hard time believing this stuff."

"I know."

"Why would magical beings have to resort to blackmail? Why couldn't they just force the rest of us to do their bidding? If there are witches, why don't they run the world?"

"They run part of the world."

I felt his stare and shrugged. "That's the truth. There are witches in positions of power. Just like there are mortals in positions of power. We're not omnipotent. We're not...we're mortal too, remember?"

"That's what you've said."

"It's the truth. We have certain advantages—"

"What are your disadvantages?" he cut in.

I hesitated. "For one thing, there are a lot fewer of us than you. We're not prolific. Few witches bear more than one child. Most can't conceive at all. In the numbers game, we're slowly but surely playing a losing hand."

He was silent.

I said, "When it comes to our...powers, they're more like candlelight than atomic blasts. That doesn't mean one couldn't achieve the same effect as punching in a doomsday code, but it would take a lot more than magic to achieve that end."

He said dryly, "I'm happy to hear it."

I closed my eyes. "This conversation makes me sad."

I could feel his eyes on my face. He said gently, "Why's that?"

"Because I know you're thinking of all the ways I'm not like you, all the ways that I'm not *human*."

John said after a moment, "But you *are* human. I know that. As for not being like me, that's a good thing. I wouldn't be in love with anyone like me. It still amazes me that you are."

I opened my eyes. "I love you more than anything in this world."

His gaze was grave and maybe just a little perplexed. "I know. Sometimes I think it must have been you who was under a love spell."

I laughed. "No. *Maman* said not, and she would know."

"Then I guess you just have truly terrible taste in men, *ma belle*."

I wrinkled my nose at the feminine noun. "You do know *belle* is for women."

"I guess. It means beautiful, right?"

"Yes."

"Then I think it's the right word."

I snorted.

John drained his glass, set it on the table, and rose. He reached a hand down to me. "Come to bed, my wicked witch, and I'll show you how much I love you."

I took his hand and let him draw me to my feet.

The bedside lamp cast its own sweet, shadowy spell of satiny light and gentle shadows. That mellow radiance caught the glint of John's eyes and teeth and hair, the gleam of taut, polished skin and hard muscles. The sheets tangled around us, a different kind of handfasting, binding us together.

Till death do us part.

John's cock rubbed up against my own, sending an electric tingle shooting from the base of my spine to the base of my skull. "Now that's magic," John's voice was deep and husky.

I sighed, *"C'est beau, mon amour"*—he had this thing about *la langue française* pillow talk—as I smoothed my hands up and down his wide, muscular back. He was so beautiful. *A lean, mean killing machine.*

My hands froze. Where had that terrible thought come from?

"Nice," John murmured. His mouth brushed mine, once, twice, thrice… Sweet, coaxing, cherishing kisses, speaking to me in our own language. "Everything about you is so *nice*."

Who would think *nice* could be such a compliment? Such a little, loving word? But that was how John paid out his compliments, these small, scattered gems. Like a dusty prospector paying for his provisions, his necessities, in tiny uncut diamonds.

His hand pushed between my thighs to caress my balls, and I groaned, instinctively shoving into his hold.

Our mouths met again in a kiss that soon grew wild, impatient. What was it when you were getting everything you craved, but it *still* wasn't enough, you *still* wanted more? John broke away to trail hot, hungry kisses down my throat, my skin burning everywhere that fiery butterfly lit.

"How is it possible to love someone this much?" he whispered, and he sounded truly bewildered.

"Comment remets-tu en question l'amour?" That was not pillow talk; that was genuine puzzlement. How do you question love? *Why* would you question love? "Is it not like questioning oxygen?"

"More like questioning fire," he muttered.

His hand found and stroked my cock—already as thick and straight as a witch's staff—painfully hard, painfully rigid, close to bursting with the spell it wished to cast. And as though wishing to control that power, John's hand pumped me—just once—down and up, big fist grazing my belly and then sliding up to the sensitive glans. I shuddered from head to toe. *"John…"*

His hands moved over me, urging me up, helping me into position, and it was easy and familiar as I maneuvered into place between John's powerful thighs. John's cock nudged my ass, and John spoke soft words, nasty words against my ear. I laughed, my breath caught, I laughed again.

Sex. There's really nothing like it. You say the things you would never otherwise speak aloud. You show the things you would never otherwise reveal. We are naked in sex as we are naked nowhere else.

He said, "There are days when it's all I can do to concentrate on anything but *this*." His cock scraped lightly down the crack of my ass, seeking entrance, trying for that opening spell.

"But of course," I said. "This is yours. I am yours. As you are mine." *So mote it be.*

I couldn't help the instinctive arch as John's thick cock pushed into my body, piercing me, but slowly, savoringly, John's breath catching, his heart thumping against my shoulder blades.

"Jesus. God. Cosmo…" His voice was rough, unsteady.

I uttered a throaty moan of stung pleasure.

John responded instantly, unleashed, thrusting in fierce, deep strokes, and I slammed back against him. For a few seconds it was simply fucking, something more like a fight than making love. Both of us shoving, crowding, insisting *I must have this…*

But then the tempo changed, the emotional tempo as well as the rhythm of our humping bodies, and we fell into sync, into an *after-you-no-you-first* that was more like a dance. A dance where each time we learned—taught each other—new steps.

This was the truth of coupling. Sometimes it was rough and clumsy, and sometimes it was graceful and…attuned. But so long as there was love, the physical exercise itself did not matter.

"*Parles-moi*," John gulped, and I laughed because John did not speak French and would not understand what I said, and yet he loved the sound of me speaking French.

My laugh was shaky. "*Il fut un temps où...*" Once upon a time. "*Il y avait un brave soldat...*"

John nuzzled beneath my ear, making my whole body feel flushed and damp with our exertions, and his hand covered mine, taking control, pumping my cock in hard, strong strokes, an efficient milking. Glittering drops formed at the slit of my throbbing penis.

And then John's whole body stiffened, he cried out, and I felt the jolt of his orgasm thrumming through my body, singing through me, setting me alight. I too began to come in heated, sparkling spurts.

It seemed to go on and on, and yet was still over far too fast. John's thrusts began to slow. He shuddered. Thrust against me sharply, once...twice... Shivered again.

Still joined, still one, we collapsed into the downy cloud of the bedclothes, and John's face nudged mine, John's mouth latching on, sweet, but still hungry as though it was not enough, could never be enough. My chest tightened in crazy emotional response.

My own erection was retreating fast, moving to a safe distance, and after a few moments John's stiff length softened, slipped out of my body. He pulled me into his arms, rested his flushed face against my damp hair.

"Thou shalt not suffer a witch to live."

John's eyes glowed yellow in the firelight. His smile was cruel as he watched Lachlan jab the fire, then raise the sizzling red-hot tip of the spit to my eyes. I tried frantically to pull away, but the witch collar held me fast. My screams echoed off the stones of the dungeon walls.

"Cos. Cosmo. Cos. Open your eyes."

Did I know that faraway voice?

"Cos. Sweetheart. It's me. You're dreaming."

I stopped struggling, stopped screaming, opened my eyes.

I was in bed. My bed. My bedroom. The lamp was on, light radiating off the crystal knobs atop each tall and graceful bedpost, illuminating the armoire with its carved lovebirds, the Scully & Scully porcelain soldiers at attention on the fireplace mantel, and John's worry-lined face.

John.

His chestnut hair stuck up in tufts. His eyes looked black with apprehension. His voice was sleep-roughened, strained.

"It's just a dream. A bad dream. We all have them. You're all right now." He added doubtfully, "*Are* you all right?"

I was still shaking, my body soaked in sweat, breathing hard, breathing as though I'd been running for my life. Running without stop for three hundred and sixty years.

"J-John?" I wheezed.

Relief flooded his face. "That's right. It's me. See? Everything's okay. You're perfectly safe."

I couldn't tear my gaze from his—those same fierce yellow eyes of the man in my dream.

The man in my dream? That man had been John. The hair, the clothes had been different, but the voice, the eyes, the hatred... That was John.

Had been John.

John, watching me closely, said, "What was it, Cos? What did you dream?"

"Nothing."

He looked startled and then confused. "*Nothing?*"

I sat up, pushing into the pillows piled against the brass star plaque of the headboard. "It was just a dream." My voice still sounded shaky.

"But... You don't remember?"

"No."

His eyes flickered, absorbing the obvious lie, the distance I was automatically putting between us. He said slowly, as though it was only sinking in, "Are you afraid of me, Cos?"

"Of course not," I said quickly. Too quickly.

"You are." He sounded winded. Gut punched.

And even though I *was* afraid of him, even though the dream still felt terrible and real, I couldn't bear the pain in his eyes.

"No." I reached out, my hand closing on his wrist—and his hand was ice cold. In all the time I had known him—did I even know how long I had known him?—he had always been warm to the touch, as if powered by his own internal aeolipile. "No," I repeated.

"I would never hurt you. Never."

I nodded.

His smile hurt my heart. "You don't believe me."

"I *do* believe you."

"No. You want to, but you don't." He pulled away—not roughly, not in anger. "It's... I'll sleep in the guest room."

"*No.*"

He hesitated. "What did you dream?"

I swallowed. "I don't— I can't—"

It took him a moment, but then he nodded, accepting it. "Until you can, I can't sleep here."

I let out a tremulous breath. "That—that's silly, John. You don't have to."

"Yes. I do. I can't sleep in here so long as you're afraid of me." He stepped into his slippers, picked up his robe from the back of the winged chair near the little staircase.

"Do you want the light on or off?"

"Off." I wanted the reassurance of moonlight, the shelter of darkness.

He turned off the lamp and again hesitated, a tall shadow in the light from the windows. I could feel his hurt, his confusion, his unease.

"John…"

"It's all right." His voice was calm. "Go back to sleep, Cos."

He left the room, closing the door softly behind him. I slumped against the pillows. Tears stung my eyes.

Worst of all, I was relieved by his decision.

Chapter Five

I woke to the sound of rain on the windows and the knowledge I was a fool.

The bronze and black Boulle clock on the mantel chimed the hour in silvery *dings*. Seven o'clock. I jumped out of bed and strode down the hall to the first of our guest rooms, barely sparing a glance for the blank space on the wall where the Louis XVI rococo mirror that had once imprisoned my great-great-great-uncle Arnold had hung. The mirror was now in storage and Great-great-great-uncle Arnold was only the Lady knew where.

The door to the guest room stood open. The bed was made. There was no sign of John.

My heart sank. I didn't have to check the other guest rooms, didn't have to go downstairs. I could already feel that emptiness in my chest. John was gone. It was Saturday, and he was not working, but he had gone.

My mouth was dry, my knees nearly giving out when I stumbled into the kitchen. The coffee machine was on, a folded note propped next to it.

I unfolded it with unsteady fingers.

Hope you're feeling better. I'll call you later. J. He'd added—squeezing in the words sideways: *I love you.*

I sank into the nearest chair, close to tears with relief. I had been so afraid of a replay of those terrible days after he'd learned the truth about me, when he had left me. When he had made the decision to end our marriage.

But he had not left me. He loved me. We would talk, and I would try to explain. Or at least we would talk.

The truth was, I was not sure myself what had happened. The nightmare had felt so horrifyingly real that in the panic of the moment, I had assumed it had to be more than key-lime pie on top of a tremendously stressful day. But really, the thing that makes nightmares so frightening is they *do* feel real. Perhaps my subconscious had bundled up all my anxieties and uncertainties and produced a night terror.

Or perhaps it was something else.

Something I preferred not to consider. Could not bring myself to believe.

Because the thing I did not wish to name would not be a coincidence. It would be a dreadful realigning of fate. And while, yes, Fate rests her hand on each of our shoulders, it is a tenet of the Abracadantès tradition that we control our own destiny.

I remembered the cruelty of John's face in my nightmare and shuddered. No. It could not be true.

The pet door opened, and Pyewacket slunk in, looking wet and disreputable, and I shook off my dark mood. After all, most times a dream is just a dream.

"*Bonjour.* So *that's* where you've been."

He ignored me, going to his dish and delicately sniffing the contents in disapproval.

"Cat does not live by paté alone."

Pye's meow was more like a snarl. He jumped onto the table, the better to glare into my eyes—just in case I had somehow missed the message.

I laughed, bumped my head gently against his, but then remembered Bridget, our housekeeper-cum-double-agent, was due in about half an hour. "Hey. You can tell me my failings later." I scooped him up, set him on the floor, and grabbed a tea towel—which I remembered was also a no-no, and exchanged for a paper towel.

Pye was not about to settle for being dried off with a common paper towel. He slid out from under my ministrations and circled me, being sure to leave his little muddy footprints everywhere.

"Thanks a lot," I muttered, swabbing hastily at the floor. "Don't take your bad temper out on me. I don't know what you expected. She's just a cat. Of course she doesn't understand."

To which Pye pointed out some uncomfortable comparisons—loudly—and sprang away to disappear upstairs.

I followed him, but it was only to shower and dress. I had been planning to go to a couple of yard sales that morning, but I was guessing that the rain had washed out that possibility. I decided instead to visit my mother, the Duchess.

I'm not being a smart-ass. My mother is Estelle Saville, Duchesse d'Abracadantès. As the favorite niece of the elderly and powerful Laure d'Estrées, she's next in line for accession to the seat of the Crone, which some would refer to as Queen of Witches.

It's kind of a misnomer because every tradition has its Queen. In fact, Wiccans use the term too, but, yes, Maman will eventually be the queen of the oldest and most powerful of Craft traditions.

Which presents its complications.

Still, life *is* complicated. Is it not?

I found my mother still *en déshabillé* in the morning room of her Nob Hill mansion, having breakfast with Jinx.

"Cosmo, *mon chou*. You are just in time. Sit down. Marthe, bring Cosmo coffee and scrambled eggs."

In that frothy blue nightie, Maman looked just a bit like a she-devil popping her head out of a cloud. I would not say that my mother is beautiful, exactly, given that she looks uncannily like the Disney cartoon version of Maleficent. She is tall and elegantly slender. Her hair is dark and her eyes green. I am told I look like her, though my eyes are gray.

"Just coffee, *s'il vous plaît*."

Marthe nodded. She has been with my mother since they were both in their twenties. I knew that in short order I would be eating scrambled eggs for breakfast.

"Hey, Cos," Jinx greeted me as I took the seat across from her. "Long time no see."

Jinx wore a man's red plaid bathrobe and raggedy bunny slippers, which made me think John's fear my mother might have too much influence on his sister was premature.

"Hello, you." I can't deny, the sudden memory of those graphic black-and-white photos made me a tad uncomfortable. Talk about TMI. "What have you been up to?"

"A little of this, a little of that." Jinx grinned. "I'm helping the Duchess with her book about Françoise-Athénaïs de Rochechouart, Marquise de Montespan. Did you know she has a book deal?"

"She…"

My mother gazed approvingly at Jinx. "She is a useful child, this one."

"You have a book deal?"

Maman lifted her shoulder negligently. It's a very French gesture. Very *c'est la vie*. "Does not everyone?"

Well, no. In fact, my father had been trying to get a book deal for the last two years. Which my mother was well aware of.

My mother sipped her coffee, considered me. "To what do we owe this honor, Cosmo?"

"I need to speak to you privately, Jinx, but first I have to ask your advice, Maman."

"Divorce him immediately. That is my advice," my mother replied. "I will pay all your legal expenses."

Jinx giggled.

"Don't encourage her," I told her. I shook my head at my mother. "I'm being serious."

"Darling boy, so am I."

Marthe appeared with scrambled eggs seasoned with fresh herbs and truffle, crisp buttery toast, and very strong coffee.

"Ah, Marthe," I sighed. "You shouldn't have."

Marthe smirked.

As I ate my breakfast, I explained Ambrose's situation to my mother.

"The poor kid," Jinx said at the end of my recital, although she's only a few years older than Ambrose.

My mother was frowning. "This is quite a serious situation, Cosmo."

"You don't have to tell me."

"*La vieille sorcière* does not belong to a tradition?"

"I don't believe so. The boy does not. He had no training when I took him on. He says the old woman has always been torn between the church and her natural abilities."

My mother made a sound of disgust. "She has kept this boy in ignorance, leaving him to find his own way. This is like leaving a bomb unattended and hoping it finds a good home."

"I know."

Though her eyes rested on my face, she seemed to be looking through me. "The Goddess must have some purpose in leading this boy to you—and to us."

"I hope so."

She was thoughtful. "How strong is she? How great are her powers?"

"Stronger than I would have expected in one so old. But there's a general lack of control, of focus. *Elle est folle.* I believe she would have killed me if she had been able."

"Why was she left in charge of the boy? Were there no older relatives who could take some responsibility?"

"It seems not. Ambrose's mother fell out with the grandmother for reasons unknown to me. There's an uncle, but he lives outside the States."

Maman nodded absently.

Jinx muttered, "I can't believe Ambrose is a witch and I'm..."

Not.

She didn't finish the thought, but then she didn't have to.

"The ways of the Goddess are unknowable," I said.

She gave me a *Really?* look, for which I couldn't blame her.

Maman said, "We have not yet determined your abilities, *ma petite chérie.*" She returned her attention to me. "Cosmo, this is a delicate situation. *La vieille sorcière* is not Abracadantès. She may belong to another tradition, and your attempts to help may be viewed as trespass. *Par contre*, the boy is your apprentice and therefore your responsibility."

"I know."

"I have no immediate solution for you, but I can provide you with several tinctures that the boy can try. It's a risky business."

"The situation is somewhat desperate."

"Yes. I see that. *Très bien.* I will put together a...a sampler while you have your conversation with Joan." She patted her lips with the linen napkin, rose, and left the room. Her Familiar, a geriatric raven by the name of Horatio, flew from his perch to land on her shoulder as she swept out.

As the tall door swung shut, Jinx turned to me. Her eyes were shining. "I love her. I wish she were my mother."

Having suffered through a number of Friday dinners with Nola, I couldn't fault her for that. John and I still had at least seven messages from Nola on our home answering machine, all of them to do with Jinx.

"She's definitely taken to you," I said.

"So what's going on? Why are you being so secretive?"

I cleared my throat. "It's a little awkward. I don't mean to embarrass you." I began with the arrival of the compromising photos in the mail. By the end of my story, she was laughing.

"Oh my God. Poor John. He must have just about had a stroke."

That kind of irritated me, to be honest. "I think he was concerned that you might have feelings for the guy in the photos. Because John's pretty sure he must be involved."

Jinx rolled her eyes. "*Of course* he is. Because he's totally paranoid. I can guarantee that Eddie is not part of some giant blackmail conspiracy." She made a disgusted sound.

"That's good. Are you and Eddie still…?"

"No. That was eons ago."

"Before John and I met?"

She hesitated, thinking. "No. No, I think it was maybe around the same time?" She brightened. "I remember. It was while you guys were on your honeymoon. I met him at Death Guild. Eddie said he was a friend of a friend of yours."

"A friend of a friend? What friend?"

She wrinkled her forehead. "Roy? Ray? I can't remember. I just remember this person was in the hospital in a coma after someone ran them down one night."

I stared at her. "*Rex?*"

Jinx smiled. "That was it. Rex. Anyway, he seemed like a nice enough guy. Eddie, I mean." She shrugged.

I doubted it. But maybe living with John was making me paranoid too.

"It's definitely over between you?"

"*Yes*, Cos. He turned out to be just another poser." She made a face. "You can reassure John that I'm not dating a blackmailer or getting engaged to a petty criminal."

"What's his last name?"

"Darksoul. I doubt it's his real name."

"Uh, yeah. Eddie Darksoul? Seems unlikely. Do you have any idea where he lives?"

"I know where he lived *then*. An apartment on Broadway Street. He could have moved. Who knows?" She added, "You could tell John that not every single person who meets me is only trying to get close to *him*."

"Just the opposite, I'd think."

"*Exactly.*"

"John's a little overprotective. That's all. He loves you. He's concerned for you."

She curled her lip. "You keep telling yourself that, Cos. One of these days you're going to figure it out. John's controlling and domineering and a bully."

"I don't think that's fair."

"You don't know him like I know him."

I was silent for a moment. "John thinks he knows you too. Do you think he sees the whole picture?"

"Of course not. Not even close."

"Don't you think it maybe goes both ways?"

"Nope." She studied me. "Sorry. I know you're still crazy about him. And I will say, he's different with you. But people don't change."

"I don't agree. I think if people *want* to change—"

"No." She even looked a little sorry for me. "You're dreaming if you think that. Even if they were to live a million years, people don't change."

Chapter Six

I could not find anyone named Eddie Darksoul who lived in North America, let alone San Francisco, let alone on Broadway Street.

There was a gamer named eddiepurple and/or eddiepurplebum, who made YouTube videos about playing something called *Dark Souls*, but I was pretty sure he was not Jinx's erstwhile boyfriend.

There was an Edward Darquez who lived on Broadway Street, and I was on my way to pay him a surprise visit, when John called.

When his photo flashed up, my heart lightened with relief. I pressed Accept and said, "John, I feel like such a fool."

"No. Why would you? You had a nightmare. It was real. I saw." His voice was low and intimate. "How are you feeling today?"

"Fine. Embarrassed."

"No. Don't be. I'm just glad you're okay now. Do you still want to go to the party tonight?"

Not really. We hadn't had a Saturday night at home in nearly two months. But this party was being thrown by the mayor, and everyone attending tonight would be, in John's view, *important*. I said cheerfully, "Of course!"

"Because if it's too much for you right now—"

I laughed. "Too much small talk? Too many watery cocktails? I'm pretty sure I can survive a few hours of it."

"Okay." He sounded relieved. "Great. I'll see you around six. Are you a—"

I knew he was about to ask where I was and what I was doing, and I had given my word I would never lie to him again, so I cut him off quickly. "Where are you? Did you go into the office?"

"Yes. I thought I might as well catch up on some paperwork."

"I feel terrible. You need a day off."

"I'll have tomorrow." I could hear the faint smile in his voice. "We'll both have tomorrow."

"I like the way you think. Hey, I have to go. I'll see you tonight. Love you." I disconnected, then sank back against the upholstery of the Uber and exhaled a long breath.

Better to ask forgiveness than permission, right?

If Edward Darquez was Eddie Darksoul, John would not be happy with me sticking my nose in police business, but at least he would have the information he needed. And if Edward Darquez was not Eddie Darksoul, John would never need to know about my little fishing expedition.

It wasn't that I wanted to play amateur sleuth—there were few things I wanted less. But if this guy really was Craft and really was involved in a citywide extortion ring, I needed to know that so that I could bring it to the attention of the Société du Sortilège, who could then inform the hierarchy of whatever tradition Darksoul belonged to.

Not that it was the society's job to police other traditions. Such meddling would never be tolerated, except in this kind of situation where the bad behavior of one lone wolf was liable to result in exposure of Craft itself. The one precept that is universal to all traditions is the tenth: *In our silence lies our safety.*

Or as my friends and I used to joke: *First rule of Witch Club? You don't talk about Witch Club.*

I couldn't forget the scintilla of magic on the envelope I had received or the fact that whoever had broken into our house last night had used spellcraft. If witches were involved in this thing, and that seemed increasingly likely to me, it was a big fucking deal and needed to be dealt with as quickly as possible—and in-house, as we say.

It was street parking only in front of 1390 Broadway. I climbed out of the Uber, opened my umbrella, and jogged around the wet-beaded cars parked bumper-to-bumper on the steep hill.

The wide entrance to the dark-blue building was gated, and no one answered the buzzer, which was annoying. I glanced over my shoulder, looked up at the windows—most of them covered by blinds or drapes. I collapsed my umbrella, tucked it under my arm, raised my hands in front of the door handle.

"Ticktock, turn the lock."

I didn't expect any wards or protection spells, and I was not disappointed. The lock clicked over, the steel handle turned, the silver gate swung open in well-oiled invitation.

I stepped inside.

There was no one inside the elevators. I met no one on the third floor.

The building looked—and smelled—like it had been built in the twenties. Though there were thirty-six units, no one seemed to be around. Granted, it was not the weather for loitering in damp, drafty hallways.

I found #34 without much trouble and knocked on the door. I could hear rain thundering down on the roof, children laughing in the apartment on the right, and MSNBC blasting in the apartment on the left. Apartment #34 remained silent.

I knocked again.

The scent of baking pumpkin-spice muffins wafted down the chilly hall.

I was just starting to get uneasy—I've had bad experience with people not answering my knock—when the door suddenly flew open and a mostly naked man in camo briefs and an aqua gel sleep mask pushed up like a headband glared at me.

"Do you know what time it is?" he demanded.

"Just after ten, I think."

"*Ten?* Ten! I've had less than two hours' sleep!"

His hair was brown, lighter and longer than it had appeared in the photos, but judging by his extensive body art, I was pretty sure I had the right guy. The skull centerpiece chest wing tattoo was my first clue.

"Sorry to wake you. Are you Eddie Darksoul?"

His scowl gave way to an expression I couldn't quite read. He opened his mouth, hesitated, and leaned forward, peering into my face like a drunk confronted by an old acquaintance. He drew back at once, as though the old acquaintance had turned into a cobra.

"What the fuck," he whispered.

"Sorry?"

He took a step back, then took a step forward, then pushed both his hands through his hair, knocking the sleep mask to the hardwood floor. "What the fuck, man?" he repeated, only that time it was definitely a question.

I didn't have the answer, so I asked a question of my own. "Is something wrong?"

He threw me a look of disbelief, pushed his hands through his hair again, and backed up a couple of steps.

"Eddie?"

"No, no, no." He turned and began walking in a circle around his front room, clutching his head, and repeating, "No, no, *no.*" It was the right Eddie, in case I had any doubt, because I could see the Sigil of Baphomet blazoned on his muscular back as he began to make a second loop.

By then I had figured out what Jinx already suspected. Eddie was not Craft. I doubted if he was even Wicca. More likely he was just a guy with an unhealthy interest in the occult. I stepped inside the apartment and closed the door. "Hey, I just wanted to ask you a couple of questions."

He stopped and faced me. "How did you find me?"

"You're in the phone book."

He put his hand out as though pushing me back. "You gotta understand. I didn't know you couldn't swim."

I had no idea what he was talking about. I'm not a strong swimmer, but I can swim. John taught me after we had our pool installed. I hadn't wanted the pool. We had argued over having one because I had always been a little afraid of water.

Eddie was saying, "That wasn't my idea. I was just following orders."

In fact, in June, I had nearly drowned in Paris when...

I stared at Eddie. Stared into his narrow-set eyes and his pillow-creased, rather stupid face. I had the weird sensation that the floor had just dropped out from under me—or that someone had given me a shove off the embankment overlooking the Seine.

"Who told you to push me in?" My voice did not sound like my voice.

I don't know if he heard me. He was still trying to justify his actions. "It was a test. To see if you were what you claimed. But I wouldn't have done it if I'd known."

"I don't know what you're talking about," I said. "Who told you to push me in the Seine?"

"'Coz you're not supposed to tell people," Eddie said in a scolding sort of tone. "It's against the rules. But you were going around blabbing to everyone, so they wanted to know if you really *were* or you were just pretending. Because a lot of people claim to be, but it's bullshit. If you *were*, they were going to invite you."

"In the name of the Goddess, what are you *talking* about?"

He looked offended. "The test I gave you. Because that's all it was. I wasn't doing anything wrong. It's not supposed to be dangerous. How was I supposed to know you couldn't swim at *all*? I mean, you live in California."

It was not easy to unravel that tangled web of gibberish, but slowly it dawned on me that this lunatic was talking about a good old-fashioned swimming test or *test de flottaison* as they called it back in the sixteenth and seventeenth centuries. Except shoving people into a river to see what happened was not how that test was conducted.

And I guess that was the good news for me?

Because there wasn't a high chance of surviving sixteenth and seventeenth century swimming tests.

"Who told you I had to be tested?" I asked. I remembered Jinx saying Eddie had claimed to be a friend of Rex's. Rex was still in a coma, the victim of a hit-and-run that occurred shortly before my wedding to John. Had Eddie been involved in Rex's accident? Was that supposed to be some kind of test too? Did this have to do with the Society for Prevention of Magic in the Mortal Realm? It had to. It couldn't be a coincidence. What exactly had I stumbled into? What in the Nine Gates of Hell was going *on*?

"That prick the count," Eddie answered.

There were so many thoughts whirling through my brain, I couldn't even remember what the question had been. "*Who?* Wait. What count? Count who?"

"Whitney. Count Whitney."

Who in the name of the Lady and the Lord was Count Whitney?

I tried to calm myself. Tried to marshal my thoughts. "Where did you meet this Count Whitney?"

"Through friends. He never did pay me, by the way. Your friend the count. He stiffed me."

"*My* friend? What friend? Ralph Grindlewood? These friends must have names. Are you part of Valenti's coven?"

Eddie looked confused and then scornful. "Covens are for chicks. I was working with the count. I don't know anybody named Ralph, okay? I *told* you what I know."

"You've told me nothing!" I felt an expected surge of fury. "Did you have something to do with Rex's accident?"

Whatever Eddie saw in my face caused him to take a step back. "I don't know what you're talking about."

"Was that supposed to be a test too? Maybe you were trying to see if they could fly?"

Eddie goggled at me like a turkey on Thanksgiving morning, and took another big step back. So naturally I took a step forward—and pointed my umbrella at him.

"You have *no* idea what you're dealing with." I was trying to frighten him. I don't deny it. I thought it would be the best way to get answers, assuming he had any to give. He was certainly not the brightest sparkler in the fun pack.

Eddie darted a couple of desperate looks around the apartment. "I'm not dealing with anybody. I told you he stiffed me. I never saw him again."

"Did you mail me those photos of you and Jinx?"

He was already on defense and looking for a way out. That particular question seemed to send him over the edge. The color drained from his face, and he ran to the window next to the radiator, threw it open, and stepped out onto the dripping fire escape.

I followed him to the window. Ducked my head out, blinking away the raindrops. *"Seriously?"*

Eddie, crouched on the rain-slick platform of the fire escape, snarled, "Leave me alone!"

"Fine, Tarzan. I'll leave you alone. You can talk to the cops instead."

This is why interrogations are best left to professionals. Eddie was not smart, but he was optimistic. He believed climbing a slippery fire escape in the middle of a rainstorm while barefooted and wearing nothing but his underwear was a viable option.

His face twisted. He offered a hand signal that had nothing to do with the occult, backed up to descend the narrow ladder to the lower platform, lost his grip, and…fell.

Fell.

His descending shriek bounced off the canyon of surrounding apartment buildings.

I stared and stared and stared down at his splayed form in the alley below. Stared until black spots bubbled across my vision, like burning nitrate film. I closed my eyes. Blinked the spots away. Risked another look down. I had to wipe the rain from my eyes.

Eddie still lay there motionless, spread-eagled. His body would have looked cartoonish if not for the rapidly expanding red outline.

Across the way, in another apartment building, a boy of about nine was staring out the window at me.

I stared back.

He gave me a thumbs-up.

I fell back against the wall of Eddie's apartment and took a couple of breaths that did not fill my lungs. I felt light-headed. Sick. Unable to think past the horror of what had happened.

Happened so quickly. So…permanently.

Because there was no spell to undo this.

My phone rang, unnervingly loud in the empty apartment, and I snapped back to awareness of my own danger. I remembered that I could be traced through my cell signal, and turned my phone off. Too late. And it probably wouldn't have helped anyway. The bane of technology.

Somewhere outside the open window, a woman began to scream.

Chapter Seven

I stepped out of the steamy shower, starting at the sight of John standing naked in our newly remodeled bathroom.

John murmured, "Damn. I need to work on my timing," and took me in his arms. I clung to him, and his arms tightened. "Mm." His voice was a deep, friendly growl. "Warm, wet husband." He buried his face in my neck, inhaled. "I love that soap on you." I could hear his smile. It made my eyes sting.

Until that moment, the moment John wrapped his arms around me, I'd actually been... Well, not okay. Not by a long stretch. But I'd managed to hold it together.

I *had* to hold it together. There was no other option.

I didn't know if I was legally responsible for Eddie Darksoul's death, but I *felt* responsible. If I hadn't shown up there, asking questions that clearly terrified him... And what did I have to show for that fatal interview? A slew of bewildering half-answers that only left me with more questions.

But my feelings were irrelevant. Even my safety was irrelevant compared to the safety of the Abracadantès.

John nudged my face, found my mouth. I kissed him, kissed him again, again. He kissed me back, but then...

"Hey," he said softly. "What's all this?" Knowing me well enough to not mistake panic for passion.

Worse, for all I knew, somewhere in the bowels of SFPD a sketch artist was working on a composite of me right at this very moment. I had tried to do a forgetting spell on the building to remove my fingerprints in the elevator and on the windowsill. I had attempted a forgetting spell on the street to remove my image from the inevitable security cameras, but the problem was the apartment building was close to the intersection of Polk Street. There were apartments everywhere. There was a park across the street. There were restaurants and boutiques. There were cars and pedestrians. There was the kid in the window across the way. *It had been broad daylight.*

No wonder John noticed I was clutching him as if for dear life.

I raised my head, tried to laugh. "I just really, *really* missed you today."

"I missed you too." He frowned a little. "Did something happen?"

My voice wobbled as I said, "You ever have one of those days?"

"Sure. Fewer now that you're here."

I closed my eyes, leaned into him.

He said, "Cos, did you want to skip tonight? It's all right to say you need some downtime."

Yes. Please. Because what I have to tell you will not be easy. Maybe change how you feel about me. Please let me have this time with you.

I shook my head, raised my face to his, kissed him briskly. "And let the home team down? No way."

He looked uncertain—which didn't happen often—and as I pulled away, he caught my hand and kissed it.

I walked out of the bathroom. A few seconds later the shower taps blasted on again.

Sometimes you can tell a lot by the costumes people choose for Halloween parties.

For example, John wore full Highland regalia for the mayor's party: kilt, Prince Charlie jacket and vest, cream-colored hose—jewel-topped *sgian dubh* included—fur-covered sporran—whisky-filled silver flask included—and black leather ghillie brogues. From his black satin bow tie to his navy-blue garter flashes, he was the living embodiment of his own cultural fantasies.

But sometimes the choice of costume comes down to what was left on the costume store shelf. Which is how I ended up dressed as Sherlock Holmes.

When I joined John at the bar downstairs, his eyebrows shot up.

"Elementary, my dear Macduff. I waited too long to order my costume. And if you say *I told you so*, you can fix your own breakfast tomorrow."

"I always fix breakfast on Sunday," John pointed out.

"True."

"The hat—deerstalker?—is cute. You definitely have the head for hats."

I sidled onto the barstool. "Nice to know I have a head for something."

He grinned, handed me a glass of wine. "*¡Arriba.*"

"*Abajo.*"

"*Al centro.*"

"*Adentro.*" I drained the glass.

John whistled. "Thirsty?"

"Dutch courage."

He was amused. "You're not nervous about tonight? You were born with a cocktail glass in your hand."

"True. It made for a difficult birth."

He snorted.

I said, "No. I'm not worried about tonight." That was the truth. News of the death—even the possible homicide—of someone like Eddie Darquez would not have infiltrated the upper echelons of City Hall. Not yet.

John considered me for a second or two, and I knew he had questions. I braced myself. Instead, he glanced at his watch. "Did you want another?"

I set my empty glass on the bar counter. "Nope. Lead on, Macduff."

"Isn't it 'Lead on, Macbeth'?" John was setting the security system as I bade Pyewacket good night at the front door.

"No. The play is called *Macbeth*, but Macduff is the real hero. In fact, you could say he's the detective."

Pyewacket's meow was jeering. I glared at him.

We were in the car, and Ella Fitzgerald was singing "That Old Black Magic," when John said abruptly, "You can't tell Andi this, but Trace is going to ask her to marry him."

Startled out of my bleak thoughts, I stared at his profile. "He is?"

John nodded. After a moment, he asked, "Do you think she'll accept?"

"I think she loves him."

"But?"

"It's complicated. You know that."

"Yes."

"Andi doesn't believe in marriage between witches and mortals. She doesn't think it's right to spend your life with someone you have to lie to about the things that matter most."

"She'd have to tell him the truth." John's voice was flat. He didn't say it, but I couldn't help fearing the unspoken message was *Or I will.*

"She would never break her vows."

"But I thought if Trace became her beloved consort or whatever you call it, she could tell him the truth."

"Yes…" I said slowly. "That's partly true. Anyway, in Andi's case, Trace wouldn't be her first beloved consort."

John threw me a quick sideways look. "No?"

"Andi took a beloved consort in high school."

"In *high school*? She got married in high school?"

"Not married, no. But she did take a beloved consort. It didn't last, of course. It was a horrible mistake. He was half demon."

The car swerved ever so slightly.

"Wait. You're saying she could tell a half-demon the truth, but not Trace?"

"No. She could tell Trace the truth. But because he's mortal, she believes she shouldn't." John didn't like that, but it was how Andi felt. "The other problem is if Andi and Trace had children, those children would be half mortal."

"But half demon was okay?" John asked sardonically.

"No. It wasn't okay. It's one reason why she's so…such a stickler for the rules now."

"So what happens if a child is half mortal?"

"There's no way of knowing. The child's witch heritage might be dominant, in which case everything is fine."

"Is it?"

I let that go. "Or the mortal side might be dominant, which could still be okay—unless there are other children and the witch heritage is dominant in *those* children."

John didn't say anything, so presumably he understood what I was getting at. The memory of Chris Huntingdon, Valenti Garibaldi's stepbrother, was surely as fresh for him as it was for me.

"My cousin Waite is half mortal, and everything turned out fine there. Well, I mean, aside from the fact that Waite is a total di…" My voice died away.

The idea that came to me was as sudden and shocking as reaching into the darkness and grabbing a live wire.

It wasn't possible, was it? Eddie Darquez had been unwavering in his insistence that the name of the man who had hired him was Count Whitney.

Waite's last name was Whitby. My aunt Iolanthe Saville Whitby was a countess by birth, but she married a mortal commoner—Walter Whitby— so Waite did not inherit a title.

But Waite being Waite, he did still introduce himself as *Count Whitby*.

Was it possible that Eddie Darquez had confused Count Whitby for Count Whit*ney*?

"Your cousin Waite is the one who owns the Sonoma winery?"

I answered automatically, "Yes."

It made sense on a couple of levels. Aunt Iolanthe had always been a little aggrieved that my mother was born two minutes ahead of her, thus securing Maman's position in the line of succession to *trône de sorcière*; and Waite believed being two years older than me gave him dibs on eventually being crowned *L'ermite*. That's not the way it works, but in Waite's view, it was the way it *ought* to work.

My cousin had tried to drown me once before, but we had been children. Presumably, he had not known any better. This would be an entirely different thing. I couldn't believe it was true—and yet I couldn't quite shake the idea either.

John's voice interrupted my thoughts. "Did you get a call from my mother today?"

My heart jumped. The call that came through at Eddie's? That had been Nola. The woman had a gift for lousy timing. In her case, it was practically a superpower.

I said casually, apologetically, "She did. I'm sorry. I was... busy. I meant to call her back."

"No need. I spoke to her."

"I'm sorry, John. I really did mean to call her back."

"I know. It's okay." He did know. There was no censure in his tone. "It's better if she talks to me anyway."

Wise words. But I kept that thought to myself.

A giant blue rabbit was strolling into the Classical Revival mansion on Yerba Buena Island when John and I arrived at the mayor's Halloween party.

"Werewolves of London" floated on the night breeze, and grinning jack-o'-lanterns lined the brick steps as we went inside. The smell of recent rain, candles, and burning pumpkin filled the damp night air.

Mrs. Stevens—*call me Sukie*—greeted us at the door. She wore a tight black dress, scarlet-lined black cape, and a witch's hat.

"Commissioner! We're so delighted you could join us. And *darling* Cosmo!"

I'm not sure when Sukie and I got on *darling* terms, but I leaned in to kiss her and noticed she was wearing a silver inverted pentagram on a chain.

Now the upside-down pentagram is not exclusively Satanic. There are even Wiccan covens that have adopted the symbol to designate ranking. Not many. Craft does not use it, and Sukie was definitely not Craft. I wouldn't have guessed she was Wiccan. And maybe she wasn't. This was a Halloween party, and half the women in the room were dressed like sexy witches. The necklace looked old and expensive, but appearances can be deceptive. No one knows that better than those of us within the Craft.

If I hadn't already been on edge, I don't think I'd have made anything of the amulet. But after the day I'd had, I was seeing potential trouble everywhere.

Sukie led us through the giant cobweb of orange and black streamers, introducing us to people as we went. John was commandeered almost at once by Deputy Police Chief Danville and Mayor Stevens. He tried to delay the inevitable by telling them he was on his way to the bar, but Danville pointed out they were already in line at the bar, and Sukie stepped in, linking her arm in mine and telling John *shop talk* was *so* boring and she would take care of me.

I couldn't help wondering if, after the contretemps at the last party at our house—the party where I'd tried to redirect the police investigation into the Witch Killer murders—the mayor had asked his wife to keep me out of the way.

John threw me a look of apology. I tugged on my deer-stalker in my best, *All right, guv'nor.*

"You two are so adorable," Sukie said, towing me along through the vampires and witches and clowns. "He's absolutely *besotted* with you."

"He's not really the besotted kind," I felt it necessary to observe.

"He's besotted with *you.*"

We ran into Mrs. Danville—*It's Alice, remember?*—who was also dressed like a witch. Her flirty little cape was lined with orange. Her sparkly earrings were inverted pentagrams.

"Oh my God. Sherlock Holmes. That's *adorable*!" crowed Alice.

"He needs a drink," Sukie said, trying to draw me on.

Alice had hold of my other arm, and she held me in place. "Has he met—?"

"That's *next* on the agenda." Sukie and Alice exchanged meaningful looks, which made me more uneasy.

We chitchatted for a few minutes—I couldn't say about what if my life had depended on it—and then we were joined by Ann Morrisey, wife of Police Chief Morrisey.

Ann was also dressed like a witch—purple-lined flirty cape, inverted pentagram ring—and my heart sank.

Ann asked if I still enjoyed married life and whether Sergeant Bergamasco was a regular fixture in my household. I replied yes to the former and no to the latter. She asked if I had been worried to learn that Ciara Reitherman was out on bail, and I said no. I didn't think Ciara posed a danger to me or John. She asked what I had heard about Chris Huntingdon, and I said I had heard nothing. As far as I knew, he was still rooming at Atascadero State Hospital.

Ann said to Sukie, "Has Cosmo met—?"

Sukie said, "Great minds think alike!"

By now I was pretty sure who the mysterious someone the First Wives Club wanted me to meet was, and far from being pleased at the opportunity to meet SFPD's occult expert, I could feel my tension mounting by the moment.

"Are you talking about Solomon Shimon?"

Their faces lit up. "Then you've heard of Solomon?" Sukie said.

"John mentioned that SFPD has its own occult expert."

They chorused, "*Yes!*"

Ann said, "But he's so much more than that."

That was what I was afraid of.

When I had first learned of Shimon, I'd tried to Google him. Without luck. It isn't possible to use a forgetting spell on the entire World Wide Web, but witches can pay to have their internet profile scrubbed just like anybody else. The lack of information on Solomon Shimon made me think he was paying to keep his data private. When I'd suggested this to John, he'd been amused.

"You mean like you do?" he'd said.

Which...okay, yes, he had a point. The lack of easily accessible information on Solomon Shimon wasn't necessarily sinister. But it wasn't necessarily *not* sinister either.

Anyway, Sukie and Alice nodded eagerly at Ann's words.

"Meeting Solomon has changed our lives," Sukie said. "When we told him about you, he said he *had* to meet you."

I asked mildly, "What did you tell him about me?"

"That you're a witch," Sukie said. "That you know all kinds of people in the witch community."

"*Which* community?" I joked, though I wasn't remotely amused. However, it was my own fault. At the party John and I had given back in June, I had hinted at a familiarity with Wiccans and the occult that your average citizen doesn't possess. It had been for a good cause, but in hindsight, not my smartest move. I mean, I had also joked about being pregnant, and no one took that seriously. But it seemed my intimations of arcane knowledge had fallen on more fertile ground.

"How did this, er, meeting of minds happen?" I inquired.

Sukie said, "Solomon teaches at SF State. I was taking his course on Modern Witchcraft. In fact, I'm the one who got him the job at SFPD."

"*Ah-HA!*" I exclaimed, and they all giggled at my very bad impression of Sherlock Holmes.

"Where *is* Solomon?" Ann asked.

"I don't see him…" Alice craned her head, scanning the packed room.

"That's funny." Sukie was frowning. "I spotted him by the punch bowl literally just a minute ago." She glanced at me. "He said he couldn't wait to meet you."

"Maybe there was a police emergency." I was only partly kidding. The memory of Eddie Darquez was never far from my thoughts. I thought it was very likely that Eddie's body art was eventually going to attract the attention of SFPD's occult expert.

They smiled, but clearly Solomon's disappearing act was a disappointment. It was sort of a disappointment to me too, but it was also a relief. I felt like there was already more in my altar bowl than I could deal with.

My initial concern had been that Solomon Shimon was a Wiccan priest using his position at SFPD to gather high-society acolytes. Now I had to wonder if his sudden disappearance meant he had recognized me—and that he knew I would recognize him.

Which could mean a couple of things. Perhaps he was a member of the Society for Prevention of Magic in the Mortal Realm. I had suspected for some time that someone at City Hall was feeding information to the SPMMR. On the other hand, I only knew a couple of members of the SPMMR, so it seemed unlikely I would recognize Shimon on sight.

Which left the far more alarming possibility. That Shimon knew me because he was Craft. And that he knew I would recognize him not simply as Craft, but as someone from my own tradition.

I did not want to believe that. But the more I thought about it, the more I feared that Solomon Shimon was a member of the Abracadantès.

Chapter Eight

"Tired?" John asked on the short drive home.

I opened my eyes. "A little. Did you have a good time?" I had not had a particularly good time. It had not helped to be relegated to civilian-wife status. Not that I typically had any interest in police work. But when the police work had to do with things I was interested in, things that were most definitely my concern, then yes, I did resent being shut out.

That was not John's fault, however. Or at least, it wasn't entirely John's fault.

John replied indifferently, "Sure." *Mission accomplished.* That was what *sure* meant.

When I didn't respond, he glanced my way and said, "As soon as I can get away, I promise you, we'll go see your father in Salem."

I smiled faintly. "That would be nice. But I'm okay. Don't worry about me."

"I know you're disappointed about our vacation being canceled."

I was, but it came with the territory. I understood that. I had understood when we planned the trip that there was a very good chance it wouldn't happen.

I said, "There will be other trips."

"Yes."

I studied his profile in the light of the dashboard. "I never did get to meet Solomon Shimon. He left the party early."

John said vaguely, "Did he?"

"What's he like? What's he look like?"

"I don't know him well enough to tell you what he's like. He's about your age. Maybe a little older." He shrugged. "Average height, average build. Brown hair. Wears one of those handlebar mustaches that went out with penny-farthing bicycles."

I smiled at that description. It did not sound like anyone I knew.

That was it for our conversation. It had been a long week. We were both tired, and I was sick with nerves and anxiety. I had to tell John about what happened when I tried to question Eddie Darksoul, but I was dreading it. The very idea made me physically ill.

We reached Greenwich Street and went inside. I greeted Pyewacket, and John said he was going to check his email before bed. I carried Pye upstairs.

"I don't even know where to start," I told Pye as I undressed for bed.

Pye's advice was that I contact the Duchess at once.

"I do have to talk to her," I agreed. "But these are two different matters."

Pye was not so sure, and, naturally, in his opinion Craft matters came first.

"He's going to be so angry," I whispered.

Pye's meow was loud and emphatic.

"I can deal with that," I replied. "But he'll feel that I broke my word. I *did* break my word. It's taken so long to regain his trust, and now…I may have undone it all. I'm not sure he can forgive me again."

That being the case, Pye, predictably, advised that I keep my silence.

I can't pretend I wasn't tempted, but I knew that in John's view—in my view as well—I would only be compounding my transgressions.

When I climbed into our brass bed, I still had no idea what I was going to do, and I was sure I wouldn't sleep at all that night, but the next time I opened my eyes, John was standing beside the bed, gazing down at me.

His expression was a strange mix of longing and doubt.

I pushed up on my elbows. "What is it?"

"Is it all right if I sleep here tonight?" he asked.

I made a sound in the back of my throat—it hurt me that he thought he had to have permission. I sprang up, reaching for him. John swept me into his arms, and it was like coming home after a long and terrible separation, clutching each other as though we'd had a near miss and barely escaped with our lives. Even the reassurance of touch and taste did not feel like enough. When would this love stop feeling so…precarious?

John kissed me over and over, and I did my best to return the favor. I grabbed that staid and proper pajama shirt of his in my fist, gave it a good yank, heard John start to laugh as the buttons went flying into outer space.

"Whoa, slow down—"

"I don't want to slow down," I said. "I missed you so much."

"I know. Me too."

I pulled him down on top of me, feeling the delicious shock of that landing. His mouth, hot and sweet, seemed to be everywhere at once—the delightful burn of his lips tracing the curve of my jaw…throat…collarbone… He latched on to a nipple.

The feel of that went through my body like an electric jolt. I arched up, crying out, *"Fais ça. Oui. Encore."*

"Is that yes?" John gasped. "Please tell me that's yes…"

"Yes, yes." I writhed beneath his ministrations, his slick tongue sliding over the roughened points of my nipples. "Do that. *Yes,*" I whispered frantically, and I could feel him smiling at my responses.

He already knew the things I liked, even the things I was shy about wanting—just as I knew the things he liked, the things he preferred not to have to ask for. In just a few short months, we knew each other so well.

And yet, in some ways we still remained unknown quantities to each other. That was what frightened me. The knowledge that you could know someone's most intimate secrets, know when they were nervous, when they were self-conscious, know how to set them alight with only your tongue and fingertips, and a few months later could be regarded as a stranger, an outsider, someone whose calls were let go to message—and never retrieved.

Eagerly, I returned his caresses, trailing my fingers down his broad back, little blue sparks skipping across his burnished skin. I nipped his throat, nuzzled his ear.

John said—and the words sounded torn from his throat, "I can't imagine not having this."

"It's the same for me." I gasped as his mouth transferred to my other nipple.

But didn't the fact that we could put it into words mean that we *were* imagining not having this?

I didn't want to think about that. Wouldn't allow myself to think beyond the incandescent pleasure of touch, of skin on skin, of being stroked and petted and admired by the one I loved most in all the world—and giving the same and more in return. I could feel myself going up in a blaze of sensation, all the cells of my body sparking and catching fire.

We shifted a little, accommodating our erections. John's firm mouth traveled to my own. He tasted dark and dangerous, like shadows on All Hallows', like bittersweet chocolate and the reddest of wines. My lips yielded to the press of his tongue, and that slick, intimate nudge as he pushed into my mouth brought a groan of relief from me.

For these few minutes, I was his and he was mine and nothing could come between us.

The bed itself seemed to rise a few feet, rocking us gently, the stars peeking through the bedroom curtains and nodding to each other in agreement.

It was tempting to make it even sweeter for him, but I had sworn to never use Craft on him, and I would not do it now when there was already the deliberate movements of his hips rocking against mine. Pleasure quivered through me with each thrust. Each sway, each bounce seemed to send flashes through my belly and groin at the contact with smooth, hot skin.

John responded in kind, and again the meter of his hand tugging on me seemed to match the meter of my heartbeat, hard and measured and, in its own way, magical...

Time lengthened, curled lazily around us. A silvery haze surrounded us. My heart swelled with emotion. It was as though John and I had always been together. Always been locked in embrace. Two halves of one whole. I knew every inch of his body, muscle and bone and elegant scroll patterns of chestnut hair. Starlight burnished him to a desertscape of broad planes and subtle dips and powerful sinews. Shade and illumination. We held each other as the headboard thumped the wall, locked tight in an interlace of legs and hands and cocks as we thrust our way into the fierce, fraught pulses of release. Hot as dry ice, sudden and bright as raw moonlight.

I held him as he slept, but, if possible, my mind was less quiet than when I had first gone to bed. My thoughts buzzed, swarming without destination, agitated and fearful.

When I could stand it no longer, when I thought my heart would tear out of my throat along with the words I knew had to be said, I eased out from under John's arm and grabbed jeans and a sweatshirt that turned out to be John's. I crept out of the room, down the hall, out of the house. Beneath the dark canopy of rain clouds, I went down to the white garden.

The white garden had been John's wedding gift to me. Every detail had been planned by John. Every plant had been chosen by John. Silvery white flagstones ringed a wide border of ivory and white heirloom roses, cream and blush-edged peonies, and panicle hydrangeas. In the summer, the beds had been a riot of sweet-smelling lily of the valley, snowdrops, Queen

Anne's lace, fragrant white hyacinth, and choisya. That had been the garden in spring. But it was autumn now, and everything smelled like rain and overturned earth. The flower beds looked like graves, the vines winding around the wrought-iron obelisks were more wire than wood. Even the faux gazing balls atop weathered pedestals looked foggy and dead-eyed.

I closed my eyes and thought of Eddie Darksoul.

"I'm sorry. I meant you no harm."

Tears squeezed out from under my eyelids. I expected no answer and received none.

I prayed to the Goddess for Eddie.

I prayed to the Goddess for guidance.

But there too I received no answer.

The moon sank behind the cathedral top of tree branches. I sat in the darkness and listened to the frogs croaking and the occasional patter of raindrops.

I was still deep in thought when the scrape of footsteps on rock caught my attention. I raised my head and saw John's tall form coming down the steps.

My heart grew heavier still.

John reached the bottom of the steps, entered the garden, saw me sitting on the bench. I wondered if he was surprised to see me there or if he was past the old doubts. If the latter, then not for long. Not after he heard what I had to say.

I said nothing.

He came and sat down on the bench beside me.

He waited, and when I could not think how to begin, he said, "You have to talk to me, Cosmo. I know something's wrong."

His tone was so calm, so…normal.

I nodded. Drew in a sharp and shaky breath. "I don't want you to hate me."

He was silent, absorbing that. Then he sighed. "I couldn't hate you even if I wanted to. Tell me what's going on."

I made a sound that was not really a laugh, and said as steadily as I could, "I may be responsible for someone's death."

You would have thought that would give him pause, but John only said, "Go on."

"I spoke to Jinx about the photos, and she gave me the name of the man she was with. The relationship was over months ago." I realized I was stalling. "She knew him as Eddie Darksoul, but I was able to track him down. His real name was Edward Darquez. I went to see him."

John didn't speak.

I stared straight ahead. "I promised you I would stay out of police business. I broke my word."

"Yes."

My throat closed at that uncompromising *yes*. I said, "I know you don't want to hear my justifications—"

"Correct. I don't want your excuses. Tell me what happened."

I put the heels of my hands to my eyes, said, "I didn't get a chance to ask him about the photos because he recognized me."

I felt John go still. "Recognized you from where?"

"He's the one who pushed me into the Seine. He thought he was giving me a test—"

"*Test?* What the hell test was that?"

"The swimming test for witches."

"You mean—what do you mean? Like a ducking stool? That kind of thing?"

"I think so. He's not—was not—very astute. He was paid by someone to push me into the river to-to test me. That's not how it works, of course, and he didn't realize I couldn't swim."

"Who paid Darquez to test you?"

"He knew him as Count Whitney."

"Count Whitney?"

I nodded.

"Not Count Dracula? Not Count Chocula?"

"John—"

"Jesus fucking Christ." He got hold of himself. "Go on. Count Whitney hired Eddie *Darksoul* to test your witch powers by throwing you in the Seine. Okay. Any reason he didn't test your witch powers by shooting you?"

"I know it sounds—"

"It sounds fucking preposterous, Cosmo. Not that I should be surprised at this point. Go on. Darquez tells you he nearly drowned you, and then what? You turned him into a footstool? A toadstool? Can you turn him back?"

"He—" My voice cracked. "He climbed out onto the fire escape and fell. The railing was slippery because of the rain."

John didn't move a muscle for what seemed like a very long time. He said at last, "So he really is dead?"

"Yes. I don't think he could have survived that fall." I closed my eyes, remembering the smell of the rain and the sound of Eddie's body hitting the wet pavement. My stomach rose, and it was all I could do not to be sick then and there.

"You didn't wait around to find out." It wasn't a question.

"No. Someone saw him fall. A woman was screaming when I...left."

"Did she see you?"

"I don't know. There was a little boy in the apartment across the way. He saw me."

John practically jumped to his feet. He did a quick circle around the garden, stopped before me. "Don't lie to me," he warned. "Did you cause Darquez to fall?"

"*No.* I swear I never touched him."

"Did you use your...your magical powers on him?"

"No. I pointed my umbrella at him. I said he didn't know who he was dealing with. I was trying to frighten him, yes, but not... I didn't...wouldn't. I told him to come back inside."

John said nothing. His tall, silent shadow staring down at me raised the hair on the back of my neck.

"It was when I asked him if he had anything to do with Rex's accident that he started to freak out. I asked about Rex and he denied it, then I asked if he had sent the photos of him and Jinx to me, and that's when he tried to get away down the fire escape."

"You never touched him. You never did *anything*—"

"John, I never laid a hand on him. Never spoke a word against him. I give you my word."

"What good is that?" His voice was raw with pain. "Your word means nothing, Cosmo. You've promised again and again that you would not involve yourself in police business. That you would not use magic. I can't believe anything you say. *I can't trust you!*"

I rose too. "You're not the only one I owe allegiance to!"

He was close enough to punch. Close enough to kiss. I wanted to do both. I knew I would do neither.

Into his startled silence, I said, "I've made other vows. And they're just as important as the vows I've made to you, John."

"You gave me your word."

"I know. I had every intention of keeping my word."

"But you didn't."

"Because it's too much! It's not fair. It's not right. I agreed that I would not use magic as a first resort, and I've tried to hold to that. I promised never to use magic on you, and I haven't. And the last fucking thing in the universe I want is to involve myself in police business. But I have obligations and responsibilities to my family, to my tradition, that I can't ignore. I didn't want *any* of this to happen. But it *is* happening. Something sinister is reaching from my world into yours. I can't pretend I don't see it. And I can't trust you and SFPD to handle it when you don't even know what you're dealing with."

I was nearly shouting, so it was something of a slap to hear his flat, unimpressed, "And I suppose you *do* know what we're dealing with?"

"No," I admitted. "I don't know much more than you do, but I know different pieces of the puzzle."

He said in that sardonic tone I had come to hate, "I can only imagine."

"Apparently not, John. Apparently, imagination is something you don't have. Or you'd realize that there's not a rule and regulation for every situation. Not every problem can be solved with a gun or a jail cell."

"This is an idiotic conversation. Do you really think you know more about *real life* than I do?"

"You're right," I said. "This is an idiotic conversation." I snapped my fingers and disappeared.

Chapter Nine

I spent the night on Andi's couch.

"The good news is, your powers are getting stronger," Andi pointed out over waffles and coffee.

"Yes. True." I wasn't quite as enthused about that as Andi, because it sort of reinforced John's accusation that I had not kept my word about not using magic. In fact, I had used more magic since my marriage to John than in the previous two years.

"Which is a good thing if you're planning to take on…"

"Exactly," I said. "If I'm planning to take on *who*?"

"Well, clearly this Solomon Shimon is part of it."

"I guess?"

"And your cousin Waite? *Could* he be part of it?" We looked at each other doubtfully.

The problem with the idea of my cousin Waite as an archvillain and/or evil mastermind is he's never really been what one would call a go-getter. And it seems to me that part of the job requirement for archvillain and/or evil mastermind is being a go-getter.

"The Goddess knows."

"Well, anyway. You can stay here as long as you need to," Andi said.

I was stroking Minerva, Andi's Dwarf Hotot rabbit Familiar. I managed a smile. "Thanks."

"Honestly, though, Trace says the best way to deal with John is to be direct and honest. Don't…rely on subtext."

I frowned. "Do you discuss me and John with Trace?"

Andi's hazel eyes met mine squarely. "Do you discuss me and Trace with John?"

I remembered what John had told me about Trace planning to propose to Andi.

"See?" Andi said. "We love each other, and we worry about each other, so of course we discuss each other with our…"

"Beloved consorts," I finished bleakly.

Andi was silent. "I don't know about that. Not for me and Trace. But for you and John, yes. Definitely. He *is* your beloved consort. And Trace says he's never seen John try so hard, care so much about anyone. And you know, according to Trace, John was pretty wild back in the day."

"Believe me, I know." I couldn't help the tinge of acid that crept into my voice. "We can't go to dinner that some waiter or bartender or doorman or valet or—"

"Ohhkaay," Andi said brightly. "I have to go now. Sundays are Buy One Get Two Free."

"That doesn't make any sense. Why would you give *two* free cupcakes?"

"We're called the *Mad* Batter, Cos."

"Oh. Right." Anyway, you couldn't argue with success, and the Mad Batter was a huge success.

"Let me know if you change your mind about staying," Andi said, and snapped her fingers.

* * * * *

Oliver Sandhurst lived on York Street in a narrow yellow-and-red Victorian with tidy hedges, bubble-shaped topiary, and a short black-and-yellow wrought-iron fence.

I purchased Blue Moon Antiques from Oliver, and once upon a time, I'd have said he was a friend. But last summer when I had tried to petition the Société du Sortilège for help, Oliver had made some shocking statements that at the time felt like an effort to damage my standing in the Abracadantès. Perhaps I had wronged Oliver, though. He was an excitable personality. He might not have realized how potentially destructive his comments were.

The whole situation had been perplexing, given that I had not known Oliver had ascended to *le Conseil Savant.* In fact, I'd believed Oliver was on the outs with the Société after the publication of his last book.

I had not previously tried to follow up with him, but with all that happened since, I decided retracing my steps to the point where everything had started to go askew might be my best course.

I opened the wrought-iron gate, went up the red steps, knocked briskly on the red-and-yellow door with its stained-glass window.

From inside the house, I could hear Debussy's "*En blanc et noir*," so I knew Oliver was home, and sure enough, after a moment or two, the door swung open.

"Hello, Oliver."

Oliver's pale green eyes widened in alarm. He summoned an unconvincing smile.

"Cosmo, dear boy! It's been too long."

And yet, not long enough, I was betting. I smiled back. "Hasn't it? I was hoping for a word."

"I'm afraid in this case, the word would have to be no." Oliver's regretful smile did not reach his eyes. "I'm expecting company, you see. Any moment now."

"I do see," I said. "Only too well."

"I'm afraid I don't..."

"As difficult as it is to believe that you would be aiding and abetting the Society for Prevention of Magic in the Mortal Realm, given recent events, I have to conclude—"

"*I?*" Sounding truly outraged, Oliver drew himself up to his full height—which, yes, he was pretty short, so it's not like I felt threatened. "You think *I* would have sympathies with those…those nomag *barbarians*? *I'm* not the one who married a mortal. Not just a mortal, a *police commissioner*!"

He had a point—and he continued to hammer it home.

"It isn't *I* who revealed sacred truths to a mortal. It isn't *I* who revealed the existence of the Craft to—"

"I revealed sacred truths in confidence to my beloved consort."

"Who then betrayed both you and the Abracadantès!"

I flushed with anger. "By the Goddess, he did not. He did not betray me. He did not betray the Abracadantès. He's never spoken a word of Craft to anyone outside myself."

Oliver waved a knotty finger beneath my nose. "How do you know, heh? How can you know that? He is descended from witch hunters. *Nothing* is beyond him."

That stopped me cold.

"How do you know that? How do you know John's ancestry? In fact, how do you know I told John that I was Craft?"

Oliver blinked nervously. "You told me yourself."

"No. I certainly did not. I told no one." No one but the Duchess. But as much as Maman had disapproved of my marriage, I knew she would never betray my secrets.

Oliver shrugged, changed his story. "Then I don't recall. I only know this is knowledge garnered by *le Conseil Savant*. It's true, isn't it?"

There was no longer any doubt in my mind. It was as though Oliver had ripped off his kindly mask to reveal something clawed and fanged. For years, I had known and liked him, but now I saw that I had never known him at all.

"How do you know Ralph Grindlewood?"

Oliver spluttered, "He's a friend. He was my customer for many years. Now he's *your* customer and *your* friend."

"He's a member of the Society for Prevention of Magic in the Mortal Realm."

"What of it!" Oliver exclaimed. "He could also be a Republican. Or a vegan. What has that to do with anything? The fact remains that it is *you* who have betrayed your vows and your tradition."

It wasn't true, but it was painfully clear Oliver believed it was. Nothing I could say was going to change his mind, and I was still grappling with the knowledge that the only person I had told about John's bloodline was my mother. I could not believe Maman would have revealed that terrible secret. She can be ruthless, yes, but…no. She wouldn't do that.

For one thing, it would gain her nothing.

Oliver, taking advantage of my stricken silence, quoted, "*Celui qui court deux lièvres à la fois, n'en prend aucun,*" took a step back, and slammed shut his door.

If you run after two hares, you will catch neither.

What did *that* mean?

* * * * *

I knew John would not be home.

Even when things were going well between us, he tended to be a workaholic, so it was no stretch to assume—in fact, I had seen this pattern before—that, following our blowup, he would retreat to City Hall. It wasn't inconceivable that he might even move in with Sergeant Bergamasco while we figured out what came next now that I had defied his ultimatum.

I landed on our doorstep, snapped my fingers, and the front door swung open.

Andi was correct. My abilities had strengthened considerably even in the past week. I no longer had to, in the words of my mother, *sneak through back doors and scurry around the city like a common field mouse.* Now I could simply envision the place I wished to be, and, provided it was not too great a distance, make the leap.

I stepped inside, and the house was dishearteningly quiet. Bridget did not work on Sundays unless we needed her for a social gathering. I did not suppose there would be any more social gatherings in this house—which meant I would need to cancel our own upcoming Halloween party. The thought further depressed me.

"*Es-tu à la maison?*" I called to Pyewacket.

Silence.

I walked into the kitchen and jumped.

John sat at the table, drinking coffee and gazing at me over the top of the *Chronicle*.

"W-what are you doing here?" I stammered.

Pyewacket, nibbling seafood paté, hissed at me, which was unfair since I was there to feed him.

John said, "I live here."

"I thought—I thought you would be at work."

John folded the paper and set it aside. "I don't work on Sundays."

I could think of nothing to say.

John said, "When you disappeared last night, was that because you were afraid I was going to harm you?"

"*No.*"

He stared at me, unblinking, with those yellow-gold hawk eyes.

I said—admitted, "I thought you were going to say our marriage was over, and I…"

"Thought you'd leave first?" His tone was a little bitter.

"No. I didn't—couldn't—face hearing it."

He seemed to consider that. He said finally, "Till death do us part, remember?"

"Yes. I think it's more of a guideline than a rule."

He rose, went to the counter, and poured himself another cup of coffee. Back to me, he said, "I think it's a rule."

I had no answer.

"I think it's a vow we both made." He turned, and I saw he was not nearly as unmoved as I'd imagined. He was not prone to emotionalism, however. He had control of himself immediately. He held the coffeepot up. "Did you want a cup?"

I shook my head.

John replaced the pot in the coffee maker. "You can't walk out in the middle of an argument, Cosmo. That's not how problems get solved."

"I didn't— Are we—" I had to stop and try again. "I broke my word."

"Yes. You did."

"You said— I didn't think you would want to…" My throat closed, and I couldn't finish it.

John's face changed. He looked like he was in pain. He put his cup down on the counter and came to me. He wrapped his arms around me, and for a moment I was too astonished to do more than stand there as straight and unyielding as a broomstick.

"Do you not know how much I love you?" His voice was low, words spoken from the heart, words reverberating against my chest. "Do you think I could stop feeling this way because you broke a promise I forced you to make?"

"I don't—didn't—think you would forgive that."

"I'm not happy. I'm still angry that despite my repeated requests, you're involving yourself in police business. I'm angry that you endangered a police investigation *and* yourself. I feel you do bear some responsibility for Darquez's death."

I sagged against him. He said more gently, "But you didn't force him out onto that fire escape. You didn't involve him in a blackmail scheme or attempted murder. He did all that himself."

I nodded. I wished I were as convinced.

John's voice went softer still. "Cos, listen."

I'm tall, but John is taller. The top of my head reaches the bridge of his nose, so his words brushed my cheek like a kiss. "We're both new to this. Love. Marriage. We both make mistakes. We're learning as we go."

That was true. True for me, certainly. I had not thought about it being true for John.

He was still speaking. "I have a temper. When I get angry, I yell. I shout. Sometimes I say things I regret. I try not to with you. But I'm not always successful. You need to understand that just because we argue, it doesn't mean I don't love you or that everything is over. We're *going* to argue. You're just as stubborn as I am and just as used to having things your way. I'm not going to walk away from our marriage ever again. I promise you that. But you have to make the same commitment—and it has to be a promise you make because you feel the same, not because I'm asking you to."

I raised my head, found his mouth, said, "Till death do us part."

Chapter Ten

On Sunday evening John was setting up the chess board and I was experimenting with my own version of *Automne en Normandie*—substituting Calvados for Laird's apple brandy—when the landline rang.

John went into the kitchen to answer it. He returned a couple of minutes later, looking ten years older.

I put down the strainer. "John, what's wrong?"

"Sukie Stevens killed herself."

"*What?*"

"She took a bottle of sleeping pills and went out to the hot tub. When Ron went to check on her, she was already gone."

I left the bar, went to him, and we hugged. Not that we were close personal friends of the Stevenses, but this tragedy felt like it hit close to home.

"Why would she do that?" I asked.

"I have no idea."

His eyes met mine, and I knew he was thinking the same thing I was.

"Blackmail?" I said slowly.

"We'll see what the investigation turns up." He kissed my forehead. "Sorry. It turns out you're on your own again tonight."

"That's all right. I'll finish putting up the Halloween decorations. Maybe go see my mother."

He considered and discarded his immediate response, settling on, "If you see my long-lost sister, you might mention I'd appreciate the occasional proof of life."

I winced inwardly, tried to reassure him. "Jinx is okay. She needs a little time to find herself, that's all."

"Sure. I just wish she wasn't looking for herself in your mother's lair."

"I won't tell Maman you said that."

He gave me his wolfish grin and a final quick kiss. "And *you* stay out of trouble."

* * * * *

As it turned out, Jinx was not looking for herself, she was looking for my mother's Chanel tweed calfskin Coco case trolley.

"I think Phelon took it when he left," Jinx whispered as she led me upstairs to Maman's bedroom. "But when I suggested that, she went ballistic."

I whispered back, "What's going on? Where's she going?"

"She's been summoned to appear before the high council of Société du Sortilège."

I nearly tripped on a step. "What? *Summoned?* Before *le Conseil Savant*?"

Jinx nodded. Her gaze was worried. "Is it a big deal? It seems like it is. She won't tell me anything, though."

"Yes, it's a big deal. It's fucking unheard of. The favorite niece of Laure d'Estrées? The heiress to *trône de sorcière* summoned like a…a…" I couldn't think of a suitable comparison, and by then we had reached the door to my mother's boudoir.

The Duchess could be heard inside, swearing a blue streak.

I rapped on the double door frame, and my mother broke off cursing. "Cosmo, *as-tu ma valise*?" she demanded.

"Non, maman."

I'm not sure it had been a real question. She seethed for a moment, hands on hips, glaring out the tall windows at the rose garden. She said suddenly, "Joan, *chérie*, will you please now attend to the online check-in?"

"Of course." Jinx threw me a worried look and headed downstairs.

"Is it true?" I questioned when Jinx was out of earshot. "You've been summoned before the council?"

"*Oui.*"

"What's going on? Why have you been called to appear?"

Her eyes were like emerald chips. "Officially? I have been offered no reason."

"But they can't—"

She snapped, "*Bien sûr, ils le peuvent!* It's irrelevant in any case. I know *exactly* what this is. That bitch Thérèse de Darrieux. She has made her move at last. I foresaw this last summer when you told me she had finagled her way onto *le Conseil.*"

"You foresaw *this*?"

Maman waved an impatient hand. "I foresaw her end game. I did not anticipate every trivial move on the board, no."

Trivial? Being summoned before *le Conseil Savant* was no trivial thing. I couldn't think of a single instance where it had not led to disgrace or worse—much worse—for the judged.

"How can this be? What does the Crone say?"

Maman shrugged. "Your great-aunt said I must face *le Conseil Savant.*" She scowled at whatever she saw in my face. "But of course! There can be no preferential treatment in this matter. If I cannot defend myself adequately, how can I defend the Abracadantès?"

"But if you don't even know what the charges are…"

Her expression changed, softened. She laughed and came to me, put her hands on either side of my face. "Cosmo, *mon fils chéri.* You can't truly be afraid for me?"

"*Of course* I'm afraid for you! If you're right, this is a-an attempted *coup d'état.*"

She made a shushing sound. "You are too sensitive, my darling. You mustn't take these things so seriously. It was inevitable I would face rivals for *trône de sorcière*. This is not the first. It will not be the last."

"It's the first time you've been summoned before *le Conseil Savant*!"

"Wellllll… True." She made a little moue. "But I have expected this for many years."

"Then you're not taking it seriously enough. Are they using my marriage to John? Is that their excuse?"

She made another face. "I'm sure your marriage doesn't help. I suspect the complaint will center on tutoring Joan, but I doubt if it is any one thing. They will no doubt attempt to prove a pattern of behaviors that make me unfit to take the role of Crone."

My stomach knotted in alarm. "I've had it with this archaic bullshit. Dragging you to Paris without a word of explanation like you're—like it's the 1700s and you're Marie-Antoinette and they're the National Convention."

Maman frowned. "*Quelle absurdité.* That is not at all the situation. There is nothing archaic about the laws and institutions that have kept us strong and safe for centuries. It is because of these conventions that the Abracadantès remains the most powerful of all traditions."

"I'll come with you."

For the first time, she looked alarmed. "No, Cosmo. That you will not do. You must continue about your business as though nothing were wrong. As far as you're concerned, there *is* nothing wrong."

"*Au contraire, ma mère.* Something is *very* wrong. And you need some support. Especially if this is partly my fault."

Her expression was odd. She said slowly, "Cosmo, you know I did not wish for you to marry John?"

I sighed inwardly. "Yes. I know."

"So you can imagine how it pains me to say this…but this marriage has been good for you."

I wasn't sure I had heard what I thought I'd heard.

"You are happier, yes, but more importantly, you are stronger. I suppose it is having to hold your own against *un barbare* like John. It has toughened you up. If it happens that you must take the reins of the Abracadantès—"

"Don't say that," I said quickly.

She smiled. "I have no intention of allowing such a thing to come to pass. Now, *chéri*, please allow me to handle my own affairs. I have already informed Iolanthe—"

"Informed her of what? What's Aunt Iolanthe supposed to do? For all you know, Aunt Iolanthe is behind this. She's always felt she has as much right to be Crone as you."

At that, Maman looked genuinely exasperated. "I have no time to waste on such foolishness. If you truly wish to be of help, contact your father and tell him what has occurred. He'll know what to do."

"My *father* will?" You can understand my confusion. The split between my parents was not an amicable one. They are not friendly, let alone friends. However, they do—to my continual surprise—seem to stay in contact, so maybe this wasn't as unexpected as it felt.

"Yes. And take Joan to stay with you until I return."

I said reluctantly, "All right. If that's really what you want."

"Have I ever failed to communicate what I really want?"

"Well, no."

"*Exactement.* Now, darling, you must go. I cannot be distracted at this moment. Take Joan, phone your father, and keep the good thought." She kissed me briefly, then waved me away.

As I went out through the double doors, she called, "And if you see that fool Phelon, tell him I want my suitcase back."

✶ ✶ ✶ ✶ ✶

At midnight I was still awake, sitting in bed, listening to the rain and stroking Pyewacket, when John finally got home.

He checked in the doorway. "Hey, I didn't think you'd be awake."

"Hey."

He moved to the bed, leaned down to kiss me. His cheek was cold and his hair damp from the rain, but his mouth was warm.

When he straightened, he was smiling. "When I asked for proof of life on Jinx, I didn't mean you had to bring her home with you."

I forced a return smile. "Is she still up?"

"She's eating gelato and watching TV in the den." He cocked his head. "Everything okay?"

"No. Not really." I sighed. "I've been trying to get hold of my father all evening. He's not answering."

"It's the Orionids."

"It's the what?"

John loosened his tie, moving away from the bed. "The Orionid meteor showers are going on now."

"Great."

But actually, it *was* great—or at least a relief—to have an explanation for radio silence. My father was a professor of astronomy at Salem State University. Frankly, he was not good about answering his phone at the best of times. That was one thing he and my mother agreed on: that cell phones were an abomination.

I studied John's face. It was not an easy face to read, but I thought he looked tired. Then again, he had looked tired this morning, so an evening spent at the scene of a suicide would have done little to fix that.

"Was it—how was it?"

"Bad." He moved away, disappearing inside the walk-in closet.

When he reappeared, barefoot and wearing black plaid boxers, I asked, "Do you have any idea why Sukie did it? Did she leave a note?"

"No. No note."

"What happened? She seemed fine last night." Had it only been last night we had attended the Stevenses' Halloween party? It felt like the previous year.

"Did she? Because I wanted to ask you about that." He climbed into bed beside me, leaned back with a small sigh of relief.

I said, "She seemed fine to me. I don't—didn't—know her well, but she seemed excited, upbeat." I remembered all those skimpy, flirty witch costumes and the sparkly pentagrams. "I think she's tight with Ann Morrisey and Alice Danville. They might have some insight into what was going on."

He nodded. "Her daughter confirmed that."

"Oh no. The Stevenses have kids?"

"Grown and married." John was silent, frowning at his thoughts. "From what we can gather, she didn't open yesterday's mail until this afternoon. The housekeeper says there was a manila envelope in with the other things. There was no sign of the envelope afterward, and she—Sukie—burned something in the living room fireplace before she went out to the hot tub."

Guilt was a weight in my chest. "You think she was being blackmailed, then?"

"It's a strong possibility." I think John must have read my mind, because he said, "According to Ron, she's struggled with depression for some time. It's possible the manila envelope was junk mail and Sukie took her life for reasons we don't yet know."

I nodded, unconvinced. A thought occurred. "John, if you could get me those ashes, it's more than possible that I could do a spell..."

He hesitated. Just for an instant, but I saw him consider it, saw his eyes light with the possibility. Then he shook his head. My hope faded.

"Forensics has everything now."

"But if the lab can't—"

He said firmly, "I think it's better if you stay out of this, Cosmo."

I nodded. I could feel his gaze, but I didn't have the heart to meet it.

"Listen," John said. "We all have to take responsibility for our choices, our actions. But even if she was being blackmailed, you didn't send her that envelope or talk her into doing whatever she was afraid of coming out."

"Sure. But Darquez was your only real lead, and I managed to scare him into stepping out on that fire escape."

"Yeah. And that's unfortunate for everybody. But we also don't want to put undue importance on the information he might have held. We don't know. It doesn't sound like he was the kind of guy you'd want to trust with top-secret info, but maybe. What I do know for sure is, there's always more than one avenue to the solution of a crime."

I appreciated that the comfort John offered came without sugar-coating.

I sighed. "Thanks."

John tilted me a sideways look, wrapped his arm around my shoulders, and tugged me over.

Pyewacket, repositioning himself in the window seat, began to purr.

Chapter Eleven

So that was the weekend—and then came Monday.

Cold, wet, foggy Monday.

On the bright side, Blanche showed up with a box of donuts from Donut Farm, Ambrose showed up and I was able to hand over Maman's box of charms and potions, and my father finally returned my increasingly frantic phone calls.

"What's the urgency, Cosmo?" Father demanded. "Make it quick." His voice sounded small and very far away. In the distance I could hear a female voice issuing dictates from on high.

"Are you in an airport?" I asked.

"I'm at Boston Logan. My flight is about to board."

"Are you on your way to Paris?"

"Of course. What is it you need?"

"Maman instructed me to tell you she's been summoned before *le Conseil Savant*."

My father, not known for his patience, roared, "I know all that! Does the woman think I live in a cave?"

Welllll... She's more than once suggested he has the manners of a bear, so perhaps.

I opted for diplomacy. "She said you would know what to do."

"Yes. I know what to do," my father shouted. "Not miss my flight!"

Presumably, he just clicked off, but it sounded like he slammed down the phone—or possibly blew up the entire network.

I was enjoying my second orange creamsicle donut and studying SF State's schedule of courses—Solomon Shimon did not have any Monday classes or office hours—when Andi phoned.

"How did it go yesterday?" Her tone was tentative.

I was glad to be able to reassure her. "It was good. We talked. Really talked. I finally feel like maybe I'm not still on probation."

"*Probation?*" She was instantly offended, and I understood that.

"Maybe that's the wrong word. I believe John really does accept me as I am. I know now that he's not going to walk out the minute I screw up."

Really, she didn't like that a whole heck of a lot better, and I understood that too, but it was also the truth that for the first time in my marriage to John, I didn't feel like he loved me *in spite of* who and what I was.

I hadn't realized how dark a shadow my insecurity had cast until this morning. Despite the gloomy weather and the alarming rate at which my assorted worries were piling up, I felt an unfamiliar sense of peace. Of certainty.

At least where John and I were concerned.

"I have news too," Andy said a little ominously.

"Oh?"

"Trace asked me to marry him last night."

I said carefully, "But you knew that was coming."

Her voice shot up in very un-Andi-like agitation. "Not this soon I didn't!"

I winced. "You guys have been dating steadily as long as John and I have been married."

"That's not that long, Cosmo!"

"Okay. Well. True. But you love him, right?"

"That's beside the point!" Her voice wobbled dangerously. "You know it's beside the point. You know my feelings about…" Andi's voice cracked.

I felt her pain like my own. I still tried to argue. "How can it be beside the point?"

"Love is not the most important thing in the world!"

"Then what is?"

"How should I know! Duty. Honor. Tradition. We've taken our vows to put the needs of the sacred circle above the needs of the one."

"Andi, there is nowhere in the Ten Precepts that says we can't marry a mortal. In fact, it used to not be that uncommon."

"Used to not be *that* uncommon is not common! We don't live in the fifteenth century. It's not common now. I can't marry someone I'm going to have to spend my entire life lying to. I can't do that. I won't do that."

"You could try telling him the truth."

She gasped. "*Really*, Cos? *You* of all people?" and hung up on me.

Strike two. My best friend thought I was an insensitive jerk, and I couldn't pay a visit to Solomon Shimon until tomorrow at the earliest. I decided to concentrate on something I *could* control, and spent the morning paying invoices, returning customer phone calls, checking the newspapers for upcoming estate sales, and selecting a few of our own treasures for markdown.

From my office I could hear customers come and go, hear the occasional comforting chime of the antique cash register, hear Blanche and Ambrose chatting companionably as they worked.

At lunchtime I headed over to Our Lady of the Green Veil to continue reading *The Lady in the Lake*—Raymond Chandler, not Lord Tennyson—to my friend Rex who was still in a coma after falling victim to a hit-and-run in early June. The accident—if it was an accident—had occurred the night of my wedding rehearsal dinner. A street person claimed that a black Mercedes Benz had deliberately run Rex down, but there had been no corroborating witnesses, and without a license plate number or a description of the driver, the police had made no progress on the case.

Although I'd known Rex for years and we'd traveled around Europe together after I'd graduated from college, I'd had no idea they were a private investigator until the accident. Rex had no romantic or business partner to tell us what they had been working on, so it was still a mystery whether the accident-that-might-not-be-an-accident was work-related. All along I'd suspected that Rex might have fallen victim to the Society for Prevention of Magic in the Mortal Realm, but that was partly because I'd only recently learned about the society's existence, and because Ralph Grindlewood, who I knew was a member, drove a black Mercedes Benz.

In other words, it was pure speculation on my part. Lots of people drove black Mercedes Benzes, my mother included.

Anyway, four months later, Rex was still in a coma. Immediately following the accident, I and other friends had linked to create a healing sphere around Rex to give their body time to heal in stasis, but the protection of the spell had ended with the autumn equinox. If Rex did not soon awaken, their spirit would depart and their body would fade from the world.

In the meantime, all I and other friends could do was take turns sitting by their bedside, talking and reading and, yes, praying. The doctors remained hopeful but noncommittal as to whether Rex would ever regain consciousness.

I was back at Blue Moon Antiques when John phoned early afternoon to say he would be working late that night, but did I want to meet him for dinner at Brenda's French Soul Food? I did and said so, and John said he'd see me at six.

I called Jinx to let her know John and I wouldn't be home for dinner, and she said no problem, she was meeting friends.

She added, "And you can tell John, no, he doesn't know them."

"You know, he is trying," I said.

"I know. It's even more irritating."

I couldn't help laughing, though it made me a little sad that Jinx and John were still so far from détente.

Maybe it was the visit to Rex or maybe I was clutching at straws, but late afternoon, I got the sudden idea to pay Ralph Grindlewood a visit.

When I'd opened Blue Moon Antiques, Ralph had been one of my best customers. I'd eventually even come to think of him as a friend. Naturally, this was before I'd discovered the existence of SPMMR or Ralph's involvement. In fact, I had been naive enough to assume his unusual knowledge of witches and Craft meant he was sympathetic, an ally. It was galling to remember that I had talked and confided in him about Craft matters as if he had been a true friend.

Ralph insisted he *was* a friend.

But the goals of the Society for Prevention of Magic in the Mortal Realm were not compatible with the goals of Craft in general or the Abracadantès in particular.

All the same, I thought Ralph might have some insights about what was beginning to seem like a rogue witch operation aimed at harming mortals. After all, his whole *raison d'être* was to keep mortals safe from witches. And he was very much tapped into the city's preternatural undercurrents.

I told Blanche and Ambrose I'd be out for an hour or so and popped over to upper north Berkeley. Ralph lives in a renovated craftsman bungalow on Virginia Street. He works mostly from home, although he does guest lectures on the occult at colleges and universities now and then, so I knew the chances of finding him at home were high—and I was correct.

A cheery Halloween witch wreath, complete with crushed hat and crooked legs, hung on Ralph's front door. I was not amused.

Now, don't get me wrong. I love Halloween. Samhain is one of the Greater Sabbats. Halloween is a mortal holiday. They're quite different. But Halloween is the time of year when mortals seem to look upon witches with greater tolerance, even affection. Little kids in costumes are cute and what's not to love about free candy?

Ralph looked surprised when he answered the door, but unlike Oliver, the surprise seemed to give way to genuine pleasure.

"Cosmo. Come in. I was just thinking about phoning you."

"Were you?"

Ralph led the way into an airy living room with bay windows, slate-colored wood floors, and a pale tile fireplace. The house was done entirely in restful tones of gray and white and taupe—much like Ralph himself.

"Yes. I was thinking you might like to get together for drinks or dinner one night."

Ralph is a well put-together fifty. He's tall and thin and not exactly handsome, but there's something about him women find irresistible. He always has some lovely young thing in the picture and, as far as I can tell, they remain friendly with him after he's moved on to still greener pastures. His eyes are blue, warm, and intelligent. His hair's sandy and thinning at the sides.

"Maybe too soon," I said.

He looked surprised. "Is it? I wasn't aware we were on the outs."

The outs. That made my lips twitch.

"Well, you did pretend to be a friend when in fact—"

"But we *are* friends. Of course we're friends."

"It's hard to remain friends when you're opposed to everything I believe."

"Now that's not true." Ralph's tone was easy, amused. "We share many common ideas and beliefs about any number of things, including the use of magic in the mortal realm."

"Uh-huh. Anyway—"

"Cosmo, this is really troubling," he interrupted, and he sounded sincere. "I'm not your enemy. Not by any stretch of the imagination. Yes, we sometimes find ourselves on opposite sides of...of certain issues, but I believe we're more often on the same side."

"Well, if that's case, how do you know Solomon Shimon?"

Ralph hesitated, and I realized my shot in the dark had hit home. He said, "He teaches at San Francisco State. I met him when I was lecturing there a few years ago."

I smiled. "He's your informant at City Hall."

Ralph blinked but recovered instantly. "I won't deny that Solomon and I are friends, as you and I are friends. He does discuss his cases now and then. Not ongoing investigations, of course."

"Sure he does," I said. "I *know* he does. And if you're serious about remaining friends, you shouldn't lie to me."

Ralph pursed his lips, considered, and shrugged. "You're right. We shouldn't lie to each other. It's not a friendly thing to do." He gestured for me to sit, and I took my place on the short taupe-colored sofa. "Can I get you something? Tea? Coffee? Juice?"

"No thank you. I know that SPMMR has actual members of the Craft working with you."

Ralph took the chair across from me. "Yes, of course. You're not unique in your belief that magic has no place in the mortal realm. We do have allies within the Craft."

"Shimon is one of them."

Ralph opened his mouth, but I forestalled his denial. "I know he is. I know he's Abracadantès."

Ralph's pleasant expression never changed. He didn't say a word.

"I also know he's built or is building a coven of women married to high-ranking city officials, which to me seems like it would be at odds with the aims of SPMMR, but maybe not, because Valenti was doing something similar and you didn't seem to have a problem with it."

"I miss Valenti very much," Ralph commented. "She moved back to the Southland, sadly."

"Sadly for the Southland."

Ralph's mouth quirked. "Your view of the poor girl is bound to be jaundiced."

"Bound to be," I agreed. I considered Ralph as he sat there with his long fingers steepled, his expression thoughtful as he considered me right back. "I also know—well, I don't *know* this for a fact, but I suspect that Shimon is part of this blackmail scheme—"

"Now *there* you're wrong," Ralph interrupted, thereby confirming I'd correctly guessed the rest of it.

Surprise held me silent—I really had been mostly guessing—and Ralph continued, "SPMMR has nothing, *absolutely nothing*, to do with this abhorrent extortion racket. We want this person or persons caught just as much as you do. Our own members have been victimized."

"So you *do* know about the blackmail?"

He frowned. "I've just said our own members are being victimized. Naturally, *our* assumption was Craft was behind it."

"Naturally."

Ralph's brows drew together. "You're offended, but isn't that your own assumption? Isn't that what you were getting at?"

Well, yes. Except I was viewing Shimon as a renegade witch working with mortals. Mortals who I believed were most likely SPMMR. I wasn't viewing this as an official Craft operation. First of all, getting all of witchdom to work together on *anything* is all but impossible. Which is why, despite our obvious advantages, witches don't rule the world.

"How many in your organization have been victims?"

Ralph hedged. "After all, to be blackmailed, you have to have done something you would pay to keep secret. Something embarrassing or even illegal."

"Exactly."

"Not many. For *any* to fall prey to such a scheme is shocking."

"How many?" I insisted.

"Let us say…more than one, fewer than five."

"Hm." That was nice and vague. "Maybe *you* want this person or persons caught, Ralph. I don't think you can speak for your entire organization. You've been wrong before. You were sure wrong about Chris."

Ralph looked pained. "That was a very different situation."

"Not really. Witches and mortals working together to cause greater harm."

"No, but think," he protested. "Think what you're suggesting. The entire mission of SPMMR is to *protect* the mortal realm from the influence of magic. How could we then justify working with witches to harm innocent mortals in order to effect the change we desire?"

"The ends justify the means. That's not one of *our* Precepts. People manage to justify all kinds of things. You already admitted you have witches working with you."

He shook his head, and he did really seem distressed. "Working together to *prevent* harm—to prevent harm to witches as well as mortals, by the way. Blackmail isn't…blackmail is… Whoever is doing this has no greater purpose. This is extortion, plain and simple. It's loathsome criminal behavior meant to profit some evil person or persons."

"Then how do you explain—"

"A false-flag operation," Ralph exclaimed, leaning forward in his chair. "It has to be."

I didn't bother to hide my skepticism.

The term *false flags* originated back in the (all things being relative) golden days of piracy when enterprising buccaneers hit on the strategy of flying the national flag of a targeted ship until they got close enough to attack, at which time the false flag would be taken down and the Jolly Roger run up.

The idea of a false-flag operation had flitted through my mind, but I'd dismissed it as unlikely. I still thought it was unlikely.

"A false-flag operation run by whom for what purpose?"

"To discredit SPMMR!" Ralph's eyes blazed with excitement. "To turn against us those within the Craft who are sympathetic to mortals."

"I hate to break it to you: the Craft is already against you."

He didn't miss a beat. "More specifically, to turn *you* against us."

"*Me?*" I scowled. "I'm also against you."

"But you're not," he insisted. "You've been trying to live a mortal life. You married a mortal."

"Just so you know, the trying to live a mortal life isn't working out for me." It was the first time I'd admitted it to myself, but there it was. Time to face facts.

He waved that away. "You love a mortal. True?"

"Yes. True."

"One day you'll be *L'ermite*. You'll reign over the most powerful of all traditions: the Abracadantès Witch King."

I shuddered at the idea, and not just because Witch King is a vulgar term. So is Witch Queen, for that matter, but that one has slipped into vernacular.

"Maybe." I remembered the ordeal my mother was facing perhaps at this very minute, and had to tamp down that surge of instant and extreme anxiety. What if Ralph was right? What if witches were the real targets?

Except…

I shook my head. "No. Sorry. It doesn't make sense. It's not logical. *We* aren't the ones being attacked. Mortals are the victims here."

Ralph said, "That's why it's a false-flag operation."

"You've lost me."

"Well, I admit I don't see the complete pattern yet."

I sighed.

"But I know I'm correct," Ralph insisted.

"That's what they all say, Ralph. All the religious maniacs, all the persecutors of those who're different …" My voice faded as a new and alarming thought occurred to me.

I had been viewing the situation from the usual angle of mortals trying to harm witches, and of course that scenario made no sense because witches were not being harmed.

What if I was looking at this backward?

What if witches were harming mortals?

What if the plan was exactly what it appeared? That some within the Craft were tired of mortal interference, mortal persecution, mortals in general? What if the efforts of the Society for Prevention of Magic in the Mortal Realm was the final straw?

What if witches were indeed victimizing mortals? Ralph had already admitted some of the victims had been club members.

"What?" Ralph demanded. His eyes were intent. "You've thought of something. I can tell."

I stared at him. If I was right, I could not share this theory with Ralph. In fact, Ralph was one of the last people I could discuss this with. If SPMMR knew that witches were actively targeting mortals, they would escalate their efforts, and the result could be an all-out war between Craft and mortals.

Is that the ultimate goal?

Stricken, I considered this terrible possibility. What if the plan was to incite violence on the part of SPMMR against Craft? That would provide justification for something that all too many within the Craft believed already. That mortals were our enemy and we could never be at peace with them.

But there was still a big difference between never being at peace and being in a full out war.

Chapter Twelve

"**H**i there, stranger!" Our waiter—a tall, lanky blond with green eyes and dimples—twinkled down at John.

"Oh, hi…uh…" John threw me a quick look.

"Charlie," Charlie supplied. "I used to wait tables over at the Bus Stop. Remember?"

"Of course!" John lied.

"He's terrible with names," I said. "Mine's Cosmo, by the way."

Charlie threw me a distracted, doubtful look before glomming his gaze back on John.

John said, "Charlie, this is Cosmo. My husband."

"*Husband?*" Charlie repeated doubtfully. "Really?"

"Nah," I said. "I don't know why he keeps telling people that." I grinned at John. "Why do you keep telling people that, John?"

"Because you're my husband, and I want the witnesses to be able to tell the detectives who killed me."

I laughed.

Charlie managed a feeble, "Ha, ha, ha," handed us our menus, and fled.

John met my eyes, shook his head, but he was trying not to laugh. "Not nice."

"But not as wicked as I *could* be."

"That I don't doubt." His smile faded, and he expelled a long breath. "Jesus, I need a drink."

"I'm sorry. Bad day?"

His nod was curt. "Stevens wants me to fire Morrisey."

"*Fire* him?"

"Fire Morrisey, promote Danville to Chief, and if Danville can't figure out who's behind this blackmail ring within thirty days, fire him too and then resign."

"That's ridiculous."

"Is it?" John's tone was somber. "He's devastated over his wife's suicide. I get that."

"Well, sure, but it's not like the whole department hasn't made this case a priority. It's all you've talked about for the last month."

"I hope that's not true."

"Not *all* you've talked about," I conceded.

"We're not getting anywhere, though, and now this has happened. For Stevens, it's the last straw. And I understand why."

"Yes, so do I, sort of. But you inherited this police department. I don't see how any of this can be your fault."

John's smile was rueful. "Because that's what leadership is about, sweetheart. Dependability. Responsibility. Accountability."

Charlie arrived to take our drink order. John ordered a single malt. I asked if the bar could do a Black Magic martini. Charlie looked doubtful but said he would check.

"Wait. Never mind. What about an *Automne en Normandie*?"

Charlie said he would check—and departed before I could change my mind again.

I sighed, said to John, "Do you think it's weird there's been no follow-up on those pictures of Jinx that were sent to me? I've been expecting a muffled call from a phone booth every day."

"Good luck finding a phone booth. Your blackmailer's probably still looking."

"True."

"It's a mind game," John said. "They wait just long enough for you to start to relax again, and then they hit you with their demands."

"Which is usually what? Money?"

"So far money seems to be the object. We've only been able to speak directly with three victims, though." John added, "However, in your particular case, I think the blackmailer may have realized a miscalculation. Not only does my wayward sister truly not give a damn about embarrassing photos, I was never going to permit you to pay one penny in hush money."

"*Permit* me?" I murmured.

"You know what I mean."

I laughed. "Yes. Exactly what you said."

He pretended not to hear that. "Which is why I think they tried breaking into our house. They needed something better. Better leverage. Something that one or both of us were willing to pay to keep quiet."

Charlie returned with the sad news that *Automne en Normandie* was a no-go, but I had the choice of red appletini or caramel appletini. I ordered a single malt, and Charlie looked aggrieved and departed yet again.

John said, "If we at least knew how the victims were being targeted, I'd feel like we were making progress. We don't even know that. In fact, there doesn't seem to be much these victims have in common beyond being wealthy enough to pay up."

"Disposable income. Disposable time. Who does that sound like?" I knew who it sounded like to me: Ladies Who Lunch.

John raised his brows. "I'll bite. Who?"

I didn't answer because it had occurred to me that if Sukie Stevens had been part of Solomon Shimon's coven and one of his informants, it didn't make sense that she would then be blackmailed. Did it?

It didn't to me.

Which meant that Shimon probably *wasn't* part of the blackmailing ring. Which meant that Ralph was probably telling the truth about the Society for Prevention of Magic in the Mortal Realm not being behind the extortion scheme. Which meant members of SPMMR were legitimately victims. Which meant my crazy theory that someone was trying to escalate conflict between witches and mortals was possible.

Wait. *Was* it possible? Was this extortion racket really a false-flag operation to incite a war between witches and mortals? Were there really those within the Craft mad enough to believe such a conflict could bring anything but destruction to all of us?

It was not a real question because I already knew the answer.

Yes. There were.

"Cos?" John prompted. "You look like you swallowed your gum."

Now, to begin with, chewing gum is a detestable habit. I do not chew gum, and he *knows* I do not chew gum because *he* occasionally chews gum and has heard my thoughts on the matter. I opened my mouth to make them clearer still but never got the chance.

"Why am I not surprised?" a light, familiar voice interrupted.

I looked up, scowl in place. Phelon Penn, my mother's former companion, stood beside our table, glaring down at me.

Phelon and I have never been…well, at best we have tolerated each other, and at worst—which was most of the years he was with Maman—we loathed each other. Phelon is several years her junior and was one of her fencing students. He was also Abracadantès and, according to Maman, *high born*, whatever that means. As far as I can tell, he sponged off her their entire relationship.

I will grant that Phelon is handsome, if you don't mind someone with the looks and brains of an Afghan hound—also, once again according to Maman, *virile*. Which, right there, more than I ever wanted to know.

"I thought you'd decided to move to Paris," I said by way of greeting.

"Estelle is facing treason charges, and here you sit, the cause of all her troubles, eating dinner with your mortal as though nothing's wrong."

I only heard the first part of that sentence—and it hit me like a punch in the chest. "What do you mean?"

Phelon's lip curled. "As if you didn't know."

I pushed back my chair and rose. "I don't know what you're talking about."

He looked dreadful. His face was red, and his eyes glittered like he was in a high fever. "The same thing everyone is talking about. Everyone but you, I suppose."

I heard the scrape of John's chair as he also rose, and realized belatedly that we had the fascinated attention of most of the long dining room. I raised my hand, said, "*All time stop. Let nothing drop!*"

Every mortal in the restaurant—other than John—froze. A couple of witches in the corner exchanged glances, grabbed their to-go bags, and exited out the front.

I said to Phelon, "What do you mean *treason*?"

"Don't tell me you don't know she's been summoned to appear before *le Conseil Savant*."

"I know she was summoned to Paris."

"She's facing treason charges because of *him* and his family." Phelon cast John a baleful look and, unbelievably, raised his hand.

I answered with a quick, angry arc that blocked the spell before it even began. It didn't take much effort. Phelon has never been much of a spellcaster.

"How dare you?" Phelon snarled.

"How dare *you*?"

"Are you two lunatics out of your minds?" John snapped. "You can't pull this shit in public. There are security cameras. There are people walking past the windows."

Phelon stared at him, said slowly, "So it's true. He's immune to magic."

John said, "I'm immune to bullshit, if that's what you mean."

Phelon turned to me. "*You* brought this upon Estelle. *You* brought this upon the Abracadantès. *You* brought this upon all of us."

And with that, he raised his arms and disappeared à la the Wicked Witch of the West, complete with red smoke, because, yeah, he's that guy. Anything for shock value.

A very long moment passed before the last sulfurous fumes dissipated and John spoke.

"Are you fucking kidding me?" he said.

I was still rattled by Phelon's news and snapped back, "I didn't start that!"

"You're—were—going to have a-a witch throw-down in the middle of a city center restaurant?"

"I. Didn't. Start. It."

John wasn't having any of it. "But you were right there with him, casting spells and doing whatever the hell else that was."

I understood that he was angry and shocked, but it felt unfair to blame me for not letting Phelon try to kill him—assuming that was what Phelon had in mind. Maybe he'd intended to burn the place down?

"I can't just stand there and do nothing!" I protested.

John looked around the silent restaurant—silent except for the sound of sizzling food drifting from the kitchen—every single person statue-still in the midst of whatever they had been doing: forks halfway to mouths, streams of wine floating like little crimson or golden clouds, flirtatious looks frozen in time.

"Undo whatever you did," John ordered.

I sat down at the table, irritably snapped my fingers, and everyone sprang back to life. Charlie dropped the drinks tray, and the smash of glass joined the din of voices. I rested my forehead on my hand.

John sat down, glowering. "That was not okay."

I raised my head. "I don't know what you want. I *know* it wasn't okay. But what was I supposed to do?"

He didn't have an answer, of course. He continued to frown at me. "What did he mean about your mother being accused of treason?"

Unexpectedly, my throat clamped shut. I squeezed out a half smothered, "I don't know. She was called back to Paris last night. I haven't heard from her since."

"Nothing?"

"Nothing."

He said slowly, "Is no news good news?"

"No news is no news," I said bitterly.

Some of his disapproval faded. "Why didn't you tell me?"

"Because there's nothing you can do. Because if I let myself think about it, I can't concentrate on anything else." I looked away from him.

"That's why Jinx is suddenly staying with us?"

"Yes."

John studied me for a long moment. "I'm sorry. You should have told me. Even if I can't do anything, I want to know."

I nodded, wiped my eyes impatiently.

"Is our marriage—"

"I don't know. No! It's not. Laure d'Estrées, my great-aunt, gave our marriage her blessing."

"And that means—"

"Everything. Or it should."

"Okay. Well, if the problem isn't our marriage, is it something to do with Jinx?"

John remained a bit vague on why Maman had taken Jinx as her protégée. Partly, that was because neither Jinx nor I were very forthcoming about her tutelage. Partly, I believe John did not want to know. I think he hoped that Jinx was mostly there as Maman's personal assistant.

I said, "That doesn't help. The problem is, while marriage to mortals is not forbidden, it's less popular at some times than others. It's not very popular right now. And it's never been popular when it comes to *la classe dirigeante*."

"The what?"

"Let's say, the people upstairs."

John considered that, seemed to accept it. "Okay. Obviously, I don't know how this works, but I've been in a few fights over the years, and my money is on your mother. Your mom versus the Spanish Inquisition? I'd bet on Endora."

I laughed shakily. Nodded.

"It'll be okay," John said.

I nodded again, but despite his confident tone, I could see by his eyes he wasn't any more sure of that than I was.

* * * * *

Jinx was still out when I got home around eight.

I changed into silk sleep pants and kimono, fixed a cup of Sleepytime tea—no lie, it's as good as any witch's brew—and curled up in the den with Pyewacket to watch *Bewitched.* "Your Witch is Showing" is one of my favorite episodes, and between the tea and the TV, I began to calm down a bit.

How comforting Samantha's life was. Yes, Darrin was continually fussing and fuming about Sam using her powers—

actually forbidding her attending her cousin's wedding—but even Darrin usually agreed that everything always turned out for the best when Sam *interfered*.

Not that I would have traded John for all the Darrins—by the way, how did Sam not notice there were two of them?!—in the world.

I must have fallen asleep, because when I opened my eyes sometime later, the local news was on and Pyewacket's purr had turned into something closer to a yowl.

I blinked at the TV screen.

The news anchor—a concerned-looking African-American woman—was saying, "Witnesses describe the suspect as a Caucasian male in his late twenties or early thirties, six feet or taller, slender build, with longish black hair and light blue or gray eyes."

"Oh no," I whispered. "No. Goddess. Don't let this be what I think it is."

But, of course, it was exactly what I thought it was.

"The suspect was dressed in black and may have carried an umbrella with a parrot head handle."

Pyewacket and I exchanged alarmed looks as the camera cut away from the news anchor and the TV screen was filled with a black-and-white sketch of a disreputable-looking fellow with shaggy dark hair, my eyes, and an ugly snarl of a mouth.

The news anchor was still talking to the at-home viewers. "Working from eye witness accounts, a police sketch artist has come up with this composite drawing of the suspect. If you know this man, please contact the SFPD hotline at 415-553-…"

Chapter Thirteen

"*Cos?*" A soft, worried whisper infiltrated my dreams.

"Mmm?"

"*Cos, there's someone outside.*"

You wouldn't think, after seeing myself on the nightly news, that I'd sleep a wink, but it had been an exhausting weekend—and Monday hadn't proved any more relaxing. The minute my head hit my pillow, I was out.

"Hmm?" I mumbled.

"Cos, wake up," Jinx insisted. "I think she's trying to get in."

I don't care who or what you are, there is something about the words *I think she's trying to get in* that will send your heart rocketing from zero to sixty in less than two seconds. No turbocharge required.

I sat up straight before I'd even unstuck my eyes. "*What?*"

Jinx's shadowy form stood beside my bed. She gulped. "There's a woman in the driveway. She keeps coming up to our door and then wandering away. She's been out there for, like, fifteen minutes."

Heart hammering, I jumped out of bed, tripped over my boots—which was better than John tripping over them—stumbled to the window seat, and peered down.

At first, I saw nothing but asphalt and the swaying shadows cast by the tall cedars growing where the end of our cul-de-sac parking area gave way to sheer hillside.

"Are you su—"

I broke off as I saw her drift back into view. A ghostlike figure stepped back from the townhouse, raised her hands, and began to chant. Her voice was too low for us to make out the words two stories up, but safe to say, she was not blessing the house and all within.

Red sparks bounced along the woman's fingertips. She reached toward the house. Her fingertips went blue, and she staggered back.

"What's she doing?" Jinx peered over my shoulder. "What does she want?"

"She's trying to get past the protective wards." After Friday's break-in, I had renewed and strengthened all the spells and wards guarding the house.

"Can she do it?"

"I…don't think so." I wasn't one hundred percent sure, because the fact that she had shown up here at all should have been impossible.

I could feel Jinx's gaze. "You know her?"

I nodded. "I'm afraid so."

The light was poor, but the shawl, the long white braid, the stooped, frail figure were all a giveaway. It didn't make sense, though. Maman had sent Ambrose a whole chest of potions and tinctures, any one of which should have knocked GramMa down for the count.

Yet here she was, knock-knock-knocking at my door.

In uneasy silence, we watched GramMa creep up to the loggia entrance once more and then a few seconds later stumble back again.

Jinx said softly, worriedly, "We can't just leave her out there. What if John comes home and she attacks him?"

She had a point. Not so much about John. John had been as immune to Phelon's spell as he had been to Ciara's as he had been to mine. It seemed my beloved consort really was immune to magic. But regardless of John, we had a problem. Presumably GramMa would wear herself out eventually, but then what? I wasn't sure she could find her way home, and what if she ran into someone who was not immune to magic—which would be most people—and attacked them?

I would have to contact Ambrose, who was probably scouring the city for her even now. I had been so sure we had found a solution to his problem, but if anything, it seemed we had made matters worse.

This is the problem with magic. It's not an exact science.

I opened my mouth to try to reassure Jinx that everything was under control, when a tall, thin figure in black came running down the steep driveway. White tennis shoes flashed in the darkness, but otherwise the figure was indistinct. It was traveling so fast, it nearly tripped twice, but caught its balance and reached the bottom safely. The figure went straight to the old woman.

"Oh my God," Jinx said as the motion detector lights in front of the townhouse illuminated the newcomer's face. "Is that *Ambrose*?"

I nodded.

"You mean, *that's* Ambrose's grandma?"

"Yes."

Jinx shuddered. "Poor Ambrose."

Maybe that sounded heartless, but there was something very wrong with the old lady, and it was more apparent now than it had been seeing her in her usual setting. In some ways, she reminded me of a zombie, yet she *was* still human. Her emotions were unfocused but still burning bright. Was she suffering from dementia, or was the cause of her decline inorganic? Was she under a spell? Had the strain of trying to balance her gifts with ingrained religious superstition driven her to some kind of breakdown?

Neither of us said anything else as we watched Ambrose speak to his grandmother, watched the old woman seem to crumple in on herself, watched him lead her away.

As they started up the driveway, Ambrose glanced back at the townhouse and, though I doubted he could see us in the upstairs window, his expression was anguished.

"Oh, Cos," Jinx murmured. "What are you going to *do*?"

I shook my head.

Proof of how exhausted John really was, he slept through the alarm the next morning.

He was still sleeping when I got out of the shower.

I hated to wake him, but John did not approve of tardiness, especially in himself, so I leaned down to kiss him awake— and realized he was having a nightmare.

I drew back, watching his fingers twitch, his lips compress instinctively against any sound, his eyes moving back and forth beneath his flickering eyelashes. His sleeping face was pale and expressionless, but beneath that mask there was a terrible struggle going on.

It was painful to watch. Especially painful because I knew he wouldn't want me to see even this much of what he was suffering.

It wasn't the first time either.

Once or twice a month, John had these nightmares. The first couple of times, I had asked him what he dreamed. He always said he didn't remember. That he didn't ever recall his dreams. I knew that was a lie, but I also knew—believed—that I couldn't force him to confide in me.

After all, hadn't I just done the same thing to him the night before?

I hoped that as time passed, as we knew each other better, trusted each other more, he would talk to me. But we weren't there yet. However much I wished it.

"John?" I said gently.

His face quivered as though confronting some terrible pain, then smoothed out into blankness. His eyelashes stirred.

He opened his eyes, blinked at me, frowning—and then I saw recognition flood back in.

His smile was crooked. "Time's it?"

I bent down and kissed him, pressing my mouth to his, and he smiled beneath this onslaught, rested his hand against the back of my head, holding me in place, kissing me back.

When I raised my head, he said, "Good morning to you too."

"What time did you get home?"

"Three-something." John brushed his knuckles against my jaw, glanced at the clock on the bedstand, and his expression changed to one of horror. He was out of bed in one Superman-like bound.

"Holy *hell*. It's seven thirty? I've got breakfast with the mayor at eight."

I swallowed my sigh. "Will I see you for dinner?"

"Not sure. I'll call you." He disappeared into the bathroom.

* * * * *

Ambrose was about half an hour late, but since I'd been fearing he wouldn't make it in at all, I was glad to see him.

"Cosmo, can I talk to you?" he asked.

Blanche gave me an *uh-oh* look.

"Of course."

We went into my office. I told Ambrose to have a seat, but he shook his head, closed his eyes, drew a deep breath, and said, "I have to tell you something."

"It's okay. I know. Which potion did you give her?"

He sagged with relief and dropped into the plum velvet Neo-Chippendale wing chair. He put his face in his hands and whispered, "The silvery-blue one. Moon Drops, I think."

"That's mostly Valerian and dragonweed. Nothing that should have troubled her." In fact, that combination usually made for deep and dreamless sleep.

"At first it seemed like it was going to work. She went to sleep, and everything seemed fine. But then after midnight she woke up and started screaming. I tried to quiet her, and she… vanished."

His eyes were enormous and frightened. "Cosmo, if she had managed to get in… I'm not sure what she would have done. She thinks you're a demon king."

I nearly spilled my coffee. "That's… I don't get that a lot."

"She says you're— She thinks you're trying to take my soul."

A demon king determined to possess Ambrose's soul. No wonder she was afraid of me. No wonder she was afraid of my influence on Ambrose. No wonder she was determined to hunt me down. Did she realize she was using Craft to do it?

I drummed my fingers on the desk, considering this unpleasant development. "It's one of the most benign potions I can think of. I'm not sure why it would have that effect on her."

He said tentatively, "I was hoping maybe you could ask the Duchess."

"I would if I could. She's…in Paris." Both of my parents abhor cell phones, and Maman does not even possess one. I had tried phoning her Paris apartment the night before and again that morning, but to no avail. Not even the servants seemed to be home. I was trying not to make too much of it. After all, given the time difference between San Francisco and Paris, it was possible my mother had not yet appeared before the council. Heck, given the amount of luggage she carried, she might still be trying to get through customs.

"Oh *no*," Ambrose said.

I echoed his sentiment, but said, "I guess it's possible your grandmother had some kind of allergic reaction?"

It seemed unlikely, with her symptoms, but I really didn't have a lot of ideas. My strength has never lain in tinctures, tonics, potions, or philters. Those are the Duchess's specialty.

"I don't know. Maybe." Ambrose continued to gaze at me with dark, anxious eyes.

"Is the neighbor lady watching her now?"

He nodded.

"Maybe tonight try the Star Crystals in a cup of soothing tea. Dandelion is a good one."

"She doesn't like tea."

"Okay, well, try it in a cup of vegetable broth. Just whatever you do, don't use it in dairy or meat broth."

"Right. Okay. Your mom—I mean, the Duchess—wrote out lots of instructions."

"Yes, Maman is ever one for instructions." I thought some more. "I could talk to my friend Andi. She's good with cordials and concoctions. She might have some ideas."

Ambrose brightened. "The cupcake girl. Yeah. She was nice."

"She's very nice. Does your grandmother like cupcakes?"

"She does, yeah."

"Okay. Something to consider." I smiled encouragingly. "Try not to worry. Something's going to work."

Ambrose nodded doubtfully.

I knew the feeling.

* * * * *

"Consider this: the witch stereotype was created as an attempt to eradicate unorthodox practices and beliefs from Christian society. The consolidation of Christian doctrine required the creation of an enemy, and this enemy was modeled along the lines of other deviant groups, thereby justifying the persecution of so-called witches."

All around me, people were nodding and busily scribbling notes in binders—or surreptitiously checking their phones for messages.

Solomon Shimon was an Associate Professor at San Francisco State. He taught three graduate studies courses for the Classics Department: Neopaganism and Wicca, Feminism and Witchcraft, and the ever-popular Europe's Inner Demons. He also conducted a lecture series titled Hell Cop: Law Enforcement and the Occult.

Shimon's online faculty bio was free of any real details beyond his email, phone, office number, and office hours. It did offer the first clear photograph of him I'd been able to find: a color pic of a man a couple of years older than myself, with black hair, black eyes, and the most magnificent handlebar mustache I've seen outside a Victorian melodrama.

I didn't recognize him from his photo—although I had been half expecting to—but as I sat scrunched in the corner of the back row of his 11:00 Europe's Inner Demons seminar, I couldn't help feeling that we *had* met before.

And I couldn't help suspecting—given his automatic and instinctive glances in my general direction—that Shimon felt the same. But then again, that might simply be his awareness of another witch in the room.

It would make a change because, as far as I could tell, we were the only Craft present, despite the fact that every seat in the house was taken—mostly by comely young women dressed in black. Which was kind of par for the course. Literally.

"The creation of the witch myth developed slowly, during a climate of wide persecution of marginal groups within Christendom."

"Are you saying witches aren't real?" a young woman in the front row asked.

My scalp prickled as Shimon brushed that aside. "That's a whole different subject. No, our focus here today is the practical application of demonizing those peoples and cultures a society deems *undesirable*."

When Shimon spoke the word *undesirable*, he had the faintest suggestion of a lisp, and once again I felt that flicker of recognition.

Who *was* this guy?

A witch posing as Wiccan was odd enough. A witch working with the police was even odder. And, although I knew firsthand that it did happen, a witch working with the Society for Prevention of Magic in the Mortal Realm seemed the oddest and most troubling of all.

But all three of those things were true of Solomon Shimon.

He knew his stuff, and he was an interesting speaker. Ninety minutes flew by, and before I knew it, class had been dismissed and the students were filing out into the busy, noisy hallway. I waited at the back of the room—and Shimon waited by his lectern.

When the last student had disappeared out the door, Shimon turned his head, blinked, and the door slammed shut.

I came unhurriedly down the steps to face him.

"Professor Shimon?"

His brows formed a straight black strikethrough line across his forehead. His handsome mustache seemed to bristle with indignation.

He said—and now that we were face-to-face, his lisp was much, much worse, "I prefer thudents to asthk permithison before they audit my theminarth."

I knew him. I *did* know him. Who *was* he?

I said slowly, "Something tells me, if I had asked permission, class would have been canceled today."

He reared back, then recovered, sticking his face in mine and snarling, "Who in the Nine Gatesth of Hell do you think you *are*!"

My jaw fell open. The years fell away. It was second grade, Andi's heart was broken, and by the Goddess I intended to avenge her. Which I did by giving the object of her affections a green polka-dot complexion. It had taken Magistra Alizon nearly a week to reverse the spell, which had made Maman very proud—and earned me a month of after-school detention.

I won't even mention what happened when we got to the third grade and he pushed Andi into the swimming pool. Yes, witches and water have a complicated relationship. For one thing, it's the most difficult of elements to control.

"Gideon Terwilliker?"

You don't have to be related to Rumpelstiltskin to know names hold power. There's a reason every government in the world wants its citizens named and numbered, be it with tattoo, social security number, or microchip. Names and bloodlines are especially important in the Craft, so I was not surprised when Solomon—er, Gideon—leapt back in alarm, raised his hands, and began to recite a forgetting spell.

I raised my hands to fend him off and was surprised at the push of strength and energy that met my resistance.

Granted, we had all learned a few things since grade school.

As we had received the same exact early training, I went straight to ancient magic and Latin.

Autumni mensis ex illustration
Aestatis in Cantico Icon
In pythonissam potestatem de mea mendacium rune
Et noli esse stultus, qui canit tumidum super tune

His spell snapped, Gideon stumbled backward, fell against the chalkboard, and glared at me. "How dare you? You have no right!"

"You thought you'd use a *forgetting spell* on *me*?"

He stuck his chin out in defiance. "You seem to think you can usth them on everyone and everything elsth!"

Ouch.

I lowered my hands, said, "For goodness' sake. I only want to ask you a couple of questions. I didn't come here to make trouble."

He gave a HA! kind of laugh that went perfectly with his mustache. "What if I don't want to talk to *you*?"

"I already know you don't want to talk to me. It's why you ducked out of that Halloween party Saturday night. What I want to know is why?"

Something flickered in his eyes, some emotion I couldn't quite read.

"Do you know Sukie Stevens killed herself?"

He replied tonelessly, "I know."

I understood then that the emotion in his eyes was for Sukie. That meant at least part of my theory was wrong. Gideon was not the blackmailer.

"Gideon, I need help. If you're not working with SPM-MR—"

He laughed.

"What does that mean? You *are* working with them?"

"SPMMR doesn't have anything to do with what happened to Sukie."

"What *did* happen to her? Why did she kill herself?"

"None of your business. Who do you think you are? Running around pretending to be Sherlock Holmes?" His tone was scathing. "This isn't a game!"

"I don't think it's a game. And the Sherlock Holmes—" I let that go because there are things that just get worse if you try to explain them. Instead, I tried another line of attack.

"I could see that night that she was in love with you."

The pain in his eyes caught me by surprise, but he said sardonically, "They're *all* in love with me."

"Yes. I saw that too. You're their High Priest."

His eyes narrowed. "Wrong. I'm their Lord."

I found that a little shocking but did not allow myself to be distracted. "Certainly they're in love with you. But Sukie was different. She brought you the others, she got you the consulting job with SFPD, she…she gave you money and gifts." That last was a guess, but it was logical, and his instinctive flinch seemed to confirm it.

Gideon didn't deny any of it, just stood there glaring at me.

"But that made her vulnerable," I said, and I was still guessing, but I felt more and more confident as his eyes got brighter and his breaths grew rougher. "She was a target because of *you*."

He made a pained sound and turned away.

"What did they do? Send photos?" It wasn't much of a guess since that's what they had done with Jinx. If a picture is worth a thousand words, it's certainly worth a thousand dollars.

"Photos of us in the sacred circle." His voice was low, husky. "I told her it didn't matter. It wasn't important. But she was terrified of what her children would think. Terrified for *his* career. We were so happy. What did any of that matter?"

He was asking the wrong person.

"Do you know who sent the photos?"

He turned to face me. "Go away. Get out. I've told you all I'm going to."

"If you don't want the police looking more closely at you, I suggest you help me—" That was a *big* misstep.

He shot back, "Suppose the police take a closer look at *you*, Cosmo? Do you think there's a witch in the city who didn't recognize the police description of you on KPIX last night?"

"Are you crazy? That wasn't me!" I must say, it was pretty convincing, but Gideon's mouth curled in disbelief. The trouble is, lying is something we in the Craft learn practically as soon as we can speak. It's our first line of defense. We lie for our safety. We lie for our survival.

He said calmly, "Yes, it was. And we all know it."

I said with equal calm, "Look, I meant what I said. I mean you no harm. All I care about is keeping the Craft out of this."

"Good luck with that!"

That silenced me, though not for long.

"I can't believe you would align yourself with SPMMR. They're against everything we are."

"What do you know about what and who *we* are?" he demanded. "You're not one of *us*. You're royalty. You're the elite. You have all the power. You make all the rules. And you expect the rest of us to fall in line whether we agree or not."

Never mind the Spanish Inquisition. Nobody expects the French Revolution either.

I opened my mouth, but Solomon—Gideon—was on a roll. "It's the same all over the world and in every tradition. Every single one. The few rule the many. The few will do anything to hold on to their wealth and power. Well, guess what? The many are not going to take it for much longer."

"I'm not sure how eradicating magic helps the proletariat witch."

He smiled. "See? Always mocking what you don't understand. We'll see if you're still laughing when the Abracadantès no longer exists."

"I'm not laughing. I'm not mocking. I don't understand you. Why would you want that? Why would you wish for the destruction of your own tradition?"

"What has the tradition ever done for me?"

I didn't know how to answer that, so I didn't try. "How does starting a war between witches and mortals help anybody? If your plan works, a lot of innocent people—witches *and* mortals—are going to die. You teach history. You know what happens next."

Gideon curled his lip. "What *are* you talking about?"

"This war that you're trying to ignite between the Craft and mortals."

"That *I'm* trying to ignite? Are you crazy? Why would I join a bunch of disgruntled aristos engaging in a power struggle?"

"A bunch of…" I stopped cold. To say *all became clear* would be an overstatement. But a few things did become instantly, painfully clear, starting with my mother being summoned to appear before the high council of Société du Sortilège.

In fact, Maman had basically told me what was going on.

Well, no, being Maman, she had not told me a damned thing. But she had *intimated.*

"I know exactly what this is. That bitch Thérèse de Darrieux. She has made her move at last. I foresaw this last summer when you told me she had finagled her way onto le Conseil.*"*

I had called it a coup d'état, but I had not truly believed it could be that. Gideon, however, had just confirmed Maman's suspicions.

It turned out Ralph, too, had been correct. The blackmail ring *was* a false-flag operation. But the real goal was not to begin a war between mortals and witches.

Mortals like Sukie Stevens were just the cost of doing business.

The real goal, the ultimate goal, was a war between witches. Not all witches—most witches would give this little flare-up a wide berth—just the witches of the Abracadantès.

This plot hit close to home because it was at home. It was about family.

And I now had a very good idea who was behind it all.

Chapter Fourteen

When I left Gideon's classroom, I found a now-familiar figure hovering outside the Humanities building.

When I say *hovering*, I mean exactly that.

Ambrose's GramMa was floating in the air about six feet above the ground. A ring of gaping students, faculty, and security stood below, mostly taking video on their cameras.

GramMa ignored them, her glowing gaze fixed on the building entrance.

"Holy fuck," I said, ducking back into the building. I started back the other way, and ran almost immediately into Gideon.

"*Now what?*" he demanded.

I sprinted past him, throwing over my shoulder, "I'd stay inside if I were you."

"Why thsould I?" he called after me.

I didn't bother to answer. I didn't know if GramMa posed a danger to other witches. She clearly had no interest in her mortal audience, which was good news. Not entirely good news, since she was sure to make the evening's headlines. But better her than me. Despite her strength, she was so erratic and unfocused, I believed the only way she could harm another witch was if she somehow got the drop on them. And that seemed increasingly unlikely given that she shed signal like a telephone transformer about to blow.

I burst out the doors on the opposite end of the building, ran for the blossoming trees, and snapped my fingers.

I landed, out of breath and rattled, in the alley behind Blue Moon Antiques.

I mopped my forehead, opened the rear entrance, and stepped inside.

"We did have something like that," Blanche's soothing voice reached me from the showroom. "An Italian Regency apothecary chest. But we sold it earlier this week."

The prospective customer murmured their disappointment.

"However, we have a lovely little Georgian corner cabinet you might be interested in?"

My cell phone began to ring. John's photo—taken on Glas Maol during our honeymoon—appeared. I pressed the green button.

"*Hey!*" I said way too brightly.

There was a pause, and then John said neutrally, "Hey. Can you get away for lunch? I think we need to have a chat."

"Oh." I didn't quite like the sound of that—I think the lack of his usual warmth warned me this was not a casual invite. "Am I in trouble?"

"Let's just say I've been happier." His voice was pleasant enough, but my heart sank.

"It...could be difficult to get away right now."

"Try." He sounded less pleasant. "I'll see you at home in twenty minutes." He hung up.

At home?

That was not good. The privacy of our own home meant he anticipated raised voices and things being said that we might both regret.

"Cos?" Ambrose said from right behind me.

I managed not to yelp, but I can't deny that by then my nerves were shot.

I turned. "What's up?" I was smiling, but it must not have been very convincing because he hesitated.

"I'm sorry, but I have to leave. Mrs. Beverly phoned. GramMa sneaked out when she was using the restroom."

I let out a long, weary breath. All at once, I felt very tired. "Yes. I know. She was at San Francisco State just a little while ago. They have her on video. Flying."

He went so white, I thought he was going to faint. I grabbed his shoulders. "No, no, no. Don't do that. We don't have time for that."

"What are we going to *do*?" he whispered.

I opened my mouth, but the words of reassurance he desperately needed—that *I* desperately needed—were not there. I shook my head.

He swallowed hard, said, "Were you able to talk to the Duchess?"

It was hard to speak over the lump in my throat. I had left message after message on an answering machine that might never be played again. My father wasn't answering either, and that, I thought, was the worst indication of all. Once again, all I could do was shake my head.

"I don't know what to do." He sounded hopeless.

I didn't know what to do either. It was hard to imagine things could get much worse, but still I had a dreadful feeling they were about to.

I said briskly, "Listen. I think the best thing is that you go home. She's bound to show up there eventually. When she does, give her the Star Crystals in some tea, like we discussed. Don't worry about coming back here. Don't leave her alone. I'll see if I can get you some help."

"Er...sorry to interrupt," Blanche said apologetically. "Ambrose, dear, your—your grandma is here to see you."

Ambrose let out a sound alarmingly close to a shriek, and brushed past me and Blanche.

Blanche gazed after him in wonder and made the avert sign. She looked at me and shook her head.

"GramMa, what are you doing here?" Ambrose's fearful words were followed by the indistinct but querulous tones of his grandmother.

I said, as though everything were perfectly normal, "I have to meet John for lunch. I should be back by..."

Blanche was gazing in the direction of where the voices of Ambrose and his grandmother could be heard growing steadily louder.

"Maybe one," I said. "Maybe two. I'm not sure."

Blanche turned to face me, her eyes—one blue, one green—wide behind today's star-shaped glasses. "Cosmo, what is going *on*?"

"It's all under control," I assured her.

"It *is*?"

"Yes. Or...maybe not. No. But it will be."

Blanche was shaking her head. "I don't understand."

Me neither, and I, at least, had most of the facts. I gave up on the pretense that if we just carried on, we could weather the storms brewing around us.

"Listen, Blanche. Forget what I was saying about lunch. When Ambrose and *Grand-mère* leave, I want you to get rid of any customers who haven't already fled. *Left.* Customers who haven't left. Close the store and go home."

"Go home!"

"Yes. Go home. I'll let you know when it's safe to come back to work."

"*Safe?*" Blanche repeated blankly.

"Yes. Don't come back until then."

"But—"

"We'll call it a snow day."

"But it's not snowing. It's not even raining today."

"It's snowing somewhere," I asserted. "You just enjoy your extra day off. I'll talk to you soon. I hope." I pushed out the back door, started running, and snapped my fingers.

There was no sign of the limo outside our townhouse when I arrived home two minutes later.

That was good because I wanted to speak to Bridget privately.

Bridget O'Leary is our housekeeper. She was a church lady friend of John's mother, and so she'd come highly recommended by Nola, but she was also a witch and—though neither of them has ever admitted it—one of my mother's spies. That sounds like a criticism, but in fact I don't have many complaints when it comes to Bridget. She's a wonderful housekeeper and has the lightest touch with pastry of anyone I've ever known. Plus, I've come to believe she doesn't tell Maman *every*thing.

Anyway, Bridget being a part-time church lady herself, I was kind of hoping she might have some suggestions regarding Ambrose's GramMa.

I opened the front door and was relieved to hear the sound of Bridget vacuuming upstairs. My relief didn't last long.

"I appreciate that that you're on time," John's voice said from over to my left.

To which I brilliantly replied, "You're here!"

He didn't bother answering, continuing to set cartons of food out on the table in the raised dining alcove. We don't use the alcove a lot. The house has a formal dining room, which we use for dinner parties, but mostly we eat at the kitchen table or on the patio by the pool. The choice of the alcove—his attempt to find neutral ground?—made me more uneasy.

I joined him, saying, "The condemned man ate a hearty meal?"

John gave me a sardonic look. "I got you the Gladiator salad."

That was actually nice of him. I loved the salads at Heroic Italians.

"Thanks." I sat down at the table and popped the plastic lid off my salad. The scent of Italian prosciutto, spicy salami, and smoked mozzarella made my mouth water. I had thought I was too nervous and worried to eat, but I realized I *was* hungry. Maybe condemned men really did eat hearty meals?

John sat down across from me, unwrapped his OMG, and took a huge bite. He chewed, swallowed, said, "I know you didn't have time for breakfast, so eat and then we'll talk."

I nodded. This clear indication of John's obvious restraint was just making me more nervous, so I had to force myself to keeping eating.

As efficient as any machine, John ate his sandwich, drank his sparkling water, and then folded his arms, preparing to wait politely for me to finish.

I pushed my salad aside. "That's all I want. Just tell me what I've done now."

He eyed me steadily, seriously, then took out a folded square of printing paper. He unfolded the paper and showed me the composite drawing the police sketch artist had made after Eddie Darquez's death.

"Bergamasco thinks this looks like you."

I raised my eyebrows. "I don't think it looks like me. The mouth is all wrong. Do you think it looks like me?"

John said, "It doesn't matter what you think or I think, because we both know it *is* you."

I said nothing.

John took his cell phone out, pressed a couple of buttons, and faced the screen my way. In silence he watched me watching a few seconds of what appeared to be a YouTube video of a tall, skinny man with dark hair, running away from an elaborate sea-themed play structure. The tiny crew of the play structure hurled plastic shovels and buckets after the fleeing man who, fortunately, did a pretty good job of concealing his face.

"Bergamasco thinks this also looks like you."

I said shortly, "Bergamasco seems to have a lot of time on his hands. Maybe you should give him some real work to do."

John did not bother to reply. He pressed a couple more buttons and showed me yet another YouTube video. This one featured an elderly woman with a long white braid and white eyes, floating through the air, screaming invective in some unintelligible language. It was like an obscene version of Our Lady of Fátima.

I swallowed, said, "I suppose Bergamasco thinks that looks like me too?"

John continued to let the video play as he said, "As of half an hour ago, there were forty-two different versions of this on social media. In one version, a man starts to walk out of the building in front of her but ducks back inside. Bergamasco hasn't noticed him yet."

The tiny, tinny voices on the video continued to marvel at the floating woman.

"You can't blame me for *that*!" I protested. "I don't have any control over what other...other people do."

"This isn't about blame—"

"*Isn't it?*"

His eyes narrowed. "Calm the hell down, Cosmo. Unless you want Bridget to hear this too."

I laughed—which did not go over well. The lines of John's face tightened, and his eyes got that funny yellow sheen.

"It's one thing to accept that you're...different from most people. I *do* accept that."

I said bitterly, "Why, thank you."

"But with acceptance comes an expectation that you'll, at the very least, try to be discreet. *This* is not discreet." He stuck his finger in the face of the composite sketch. "*This*—" He held his phone up. "Not discreet."

"I told you about that." I nodded at the composite sketch. "You know why I went there."

"Yes. It was a bad idea then. It's a worse idea now."

"I know it. I knew it then. But it's *done*. I can't undo it."

He shook his head. "And what about the park? What was that? The witnesses claim you dropped out of the sky and land-ed on the play structure."

"Well, clearly they're mistaken."

"Really?"

"What do you want me to say? Obviously, the official version has to be that they're *mistaken*."

"Okay. And are all the witnesses who caught Our Lady of the Screaming Meemies on camera also mistaken? Because that's going to be a hard sell."

I jumped up from the table. "*That* wasn't me!"

John also rose. "But you were there."

"So were plenty of other people! Clearly."

"*You* are involved in this. Don't lie to me, Cosmo. You know who this is."

I tried to match his cold, controlled tone. "How does that— Knowing who she is doesn't make me responsible for her actions. Why are you putting this all on me?"

All at once he was visibly, unmistakably angry. "Because overnight the entire city has turned into spook central, and *you're* at the center of all of it."

It felt so unfair. He wasn't wrong, but he wasn't right either. Yes, I was involved, but it wasn't like I was to blame for any of it. Well, maybe Eddie. I did feel to blame there. But the rest of it? The rest of it arose from my trying to stop worse things from happening.

"I don't know what you want me to say. I'm trying to be careful. I'm trying to be *discreet*, as you put it. Some of this is just...being in the wrong place at the wrong time."

"And some of it is you putting yourself in the wrong place at the wrong time by playing detective."

I spread my hands. "All right. Yes. If you say so."

"Thank you. I do say so. Because it's the truth."

"I'm-I'm sorry."

"*Sorry* is not going to fix this. You're going to have to come up with something more than sorry. Because as more people figure out this is you, it's only going to get worse."

I stared at him. "Why would more people figure out that any of this is me?"

John gazed at me with disbelief. "Because it *is* you. Because it *looks* like you." He held up the sketch. "This is you, remember?"

"Yes. I remember. Is Bergamasco going to— Does he want me arrested?"

"That's the last thing anybody wants."

Was that actually an answer? I wasn't sure.

"Does Bergamasco think I-I'm a murderer?"

"No. I told Pete why you were at Darquez's apartment. I told him what happened."

I repeated faintly, "You...*told* him?"

John's brows drew together. "I didn't tell him you're a...a witch. Obviously."

"You didn't?" I felt weak with relief.

"I'm not crazy. No. I did not. I explained why you went there and what happened."

I said doubtfully, "And he believed that?"

"Yes. The forensics backs it up. There was no sign of struggle. The only witness to the actual accident said you were speaking to Darquez from inside the apartment."

I said slowly, "The little boy across the way."

"Yes. The kid said Darquez tried to flip you off, lost his grip, and fell."

I absorbed that for a moment. "But then if Bergamasco knows I didn't kill anyone—"

"That doesn't explain how you came and went without security cameras picking up your image, or the fact that you seem able to transport yourself across town in the blink of an eye, or the fact that ever since I met you, a lot of very weird stuff has been happening around town—and you're usually in the vicinity."

"In fairness, weird stuff was always happening. You people just never noticed."

"Well, we're noticing now, and it's a problem."

It *was* a problem. If John didn't have such a high profile in the community—if his work was not connected with law enforcement—it would be different. But because John lived in the spotlight, the spotlight was on me as well.

My heart began to thump against my ribs in that sickening fight-or-flight response. I tried to say calmly, "Then what are you saying? What is it you want? You said you would never walk away from our marriage again. Do you want *me* to leave? Is that it?"

"Saints preserve us!" Bridget exclaimed—and John and I both jumped.

She stood at the foot of the stairs, prim and proper in her gray skirt and white blouse, seemingly mild as milk though the gaze she turned on John was as black and hard as agate.

"Here I was thinking it was one of these home invasions we hear so much about. I never heard the two of you come in at all, at all." The *at all, at all* was laying it on thick, but Bridget is Irish and does have a little bit of a lilt.

John looked from Bridget to me and back to Bridget. I wondered if he was starting to suspect that Bridget too might not be exactly what she seemed.

He folded the sketch back up, thrust it in his pocket, picked his phone up, and pocketed that too.

"Of course I don't want that," he said gruffly, and kissed my cheek. "We'll talk this out tonight."

He turned and went out the front door without a backward glance.

Chapter Fifteen

I'd stood there stiff and straight as a mannequin, but as I heard the sound of John's Range Rover fading in the distance, I slumped down at the carton-strewn table and rested my face in my hands.

"Whisht." Bridget moved about the table, swiftly collecting the scattered cartons and bottles. "None of that. The man's mad for you. It'll all blow over by supper."

I shook my head. "John's not wrong. My image *is* turning up everywhere."

"It's this bloody technology," Bridget agreed, rather astonishingly. "You can't turn sideways, there isn't a security camera staring down your neck. I miss the old days. Now how about a nice hot cuppa? That'll put you right."

"The best thing he could do for himself is divorce me."

She sniffed. "I think he would regret that very much. Now you go sit on the sofa, and I'll be back with your tea in half a tick."

Not having a better idea, I obeyed and went downstairs to the sunken living room and dropped down on the sofa.

Bridget returned in a few minutes and set the tea tray on the low table in the living room. She poured the tea and turned toward the steps.

I couldn't help asking, "Bridget, have you heard anything from the Duchess?"

She hesitated. I knew she knew that I knew that she was my mother's agent, but it had never been acknowledged between us.

"No," she admitted.

I nodded, picked up the teacup. I took a sip of hot, comforting milky liquid.

Watching me, she said bracingly, "Don't give in to dark thoughts, sir. The Duchess is a wily one, if I might say so. She'll come through this with flying colors. You'll see."

"I hope you're right."

"You don't have to trust me, sir. Trust the Duchess." She studied me for another moment. "If you don't mind, I'll be cleaning the upper landing now."

I nodded, but the tea—which I suspected had been lightly doctored—reminded me that I'd wanted to speak to Bridget about Ambrose's grandmother. "In a moment. I'd like to ask your advice, if that's okay."

"*My* advice?"

"If that's not an imposition."

She sat down cautiously, as if she feared the chair might swallow her, but began to relax as I explained about Ambrose and GramMa.

"It's a quandary, no mistake," Bridget said at the end of my convoluted account of the last few days.

"Why do you think none of the potions and possets are working?"

She tilted her head, considering. "After all, the lad's only tried one potion so far. The Star Crystals may do the trick."

I tried to read her face. "You don't think so, do you?"

"No. More's the pity. The poor thing is slipping into the shadows."

"But *why*?"

Bridget shook her head. "That, I couldn't say. It does happen, but it's rare that there isn't some outside influence. She must have been quite powerful in her prime. Which makes her doubly dangerous now."

"That's my fear." I sighed. "All right. Thanks."

Bridget rose but then hesitated. "What other things did your mam include in the potion chest?"

"I'm not sure. It was a variety pack, for sure."

I could see her thinking this over. She said slowly, "I could pay the old lady a visit. I'm quite good with old ladies."

"I don't doubt it. I wouldn't want to put you to any trouble…"

She brushed that aside. "If you can arrange for the lad to show me the chest, I'll see what might be done."

I couldn't hide my relief. "Thank you, Bridget."

She said drolly, "Thank *you*, sir."

I wasn't sure what kind of reception to expect from Andi, but when I walked into the Mad Batter, she came around the counter to meet me with a hug.

"Oh, Cos," she whispered. "I only just found out. How are you holding up?"

Proof that John was wearing off on me, I first glanced to see who in the long line of customers waiting for their turn at the counter was paying attention to us—and it was pretty much everyone.

Andi also noticed and said, "Come into my office, where we can talk." She called to the purple-haired girl behind the counter, "Tess, I'll be in the back."

Tess waved her hand in acknowledgment.

"What have you heard?" I asked, following Andi back to her office.

I was terrified she had some new and dreadful update I was unaware of, but as she sat down at her desk, she said, "The Duchess has been summoned to appear before *le Conseil Savant*, and that the charge is…" Her voice wavered. "Treason."

"It's my fault. This is about my marriage to John."

"No. They wouldn't dare. The Crone blessed your union. Anyway, you're not the one being called to appear. This is about the Duchess."

I shook my head, but Andi insisted, "Of course it is. Cos, you can't be as powerful as the Duchess and not make enemies. They're saying this Madame de Darrieux has taken control of the Société du Sortilège, and that she's the one pushing for this."

"When I appeared before the council last summer, the membership had changed. Oliver Sandhurst was there, and Madame de Darrieux seemed to be acting as *le chancelier*, though I thought all seven members were supposed to be equal."

Andi looked startled. "Oliver Sandhurst was there?"

"Yes."

"But wasn't he banished a year ago?"

"Close. What's really confusing is he also seems to be working with the Society for Prevention of Magic in the Mortal Realm."

"*What?*"

"And he's not the only one. Do you remember Gideon Terwilliker?"

Andy blushed. "Oh. Er… Sort of."

"Well, he's changed his name and, besides working as SFPD's occult expert, he's now teaching at SF State. He's also working with SPMMR."

"I knew he'd changed his name," she said surprisingly.

"You did? You kept in touch?"

"No. No, of course not. But I looked him up on Facebook a few years ago. He'd written a really terrible book on economics and magic, and made the mistake of using his own name. It wasn't long after that, that he reinvented himself."

"Economics and magic? What would that even be? Alchemy? Pyramid schemes?"

She sighed. "I know."

"I believe he's part of this faction of witches working with the SPMMR, but with a separate end goal in mind."

"Which would be what?"

"To take over the leadership of the Abracadantès."

"Really?" Andi sounded doubtful, and I wasn't surprised because when I said it aloud, it did sound pretty wild.

"Yes. People like Gideon are more sympathetic to mortals than people like Oliver, who has turned into a raving *anti humain.*"

"Even so." She frowned. "What I don't understand is, where is the Crone in all this?"

"I spoke to Maman before she left for Paris. She said Great-aunt Laure told her she had to appear before *le Conseil Savant.*"

Andi bit her lip. "Maybe it's gone so far that even *she* can't stop it."

"Maybe." That was a horrifying thought.

"Do you know anything about Madame de Darrieux?" Andi asked after some thought.

"I think she's an old rival of Maman's."

Andi made a face. "That doesn't exactly narrow it down."

"No, I know. Here's the thing. I don't believe Madame de Darrieux is the real force behind this plot."

"You...don't?"

"No. I think she's a puppet. I have reason to believe my cousin Waite has *also* been working with SPMMR, and we both know the only reason a Whitby does *anything* is because it's to his own benefit."

"True, but talk about a puppet," objected Andi. "Waite isn't exactly the enterprising type."

"*Exactly.*"

"Exactly?" Andi was frowning, but then her eyes widened. "You mean you believe your aunt Iolanthe is behind this?"

"Think about it. Aunt I always resented that a two-minute fluke—her words, not mine—made Maman heiress to the *trône de sorcière*. She said it so many times that Waite tried to drown me when we were kids and hired someone to try again last summer."

"Wait. What?"

"Long story. But I'm sure I'm right. Nothing else makes sense."

"Well, I wouldn't say th—"

"But who else could be behind it?"

"You already admitted you don't actually know anything about this Madame de Darrieux, and she's the one who seems to be running *le Conseil Savant*, which means she's running the Société du Sortilège."

"Okay. True. But I'm very sure, for reasons I can't really go into, that Waite is part of this. And if Waite is part of this, then…"

Andi still looked unconvinced. "I'm not so sure. Regardless of the past, your mom and your aunt have been really close for years."

I opened my mouth to object, but Andi was right. My mother and her sister were pretty cozy in their own peculiar way.

"And the other thing is, yes, your mother was born two minutes early, but the Crone has leeway in whom she chooses as her heir or heiress. She didn't have to pick *either* of the Saville sisters. She could still change her mind. And your aunt Iolanthe knows that as well as anyone."

"But that just supports what I'm saying. If Maman is found guilty of treason, she'll be banished and the path will be clear for Laure d'Estrées to choose—"

"*You*," Andi cut in. "The Crone will choose *you*, Cosmo. It's no secret she adores you. Why do you think you got her blessing when you decided to marry a mortal?"

"But then that doesn't fit."

"*That's* what I'm trying to tell you," Andy said patiently. "You're missing a piece of the puzzle."

Could she be right? The plot had made such perfect sense in my mind, but Andi was correct in that the Crone did have latitude in choosing an heir. Removing my mother from contention did not automatically remove me, so if the object of all this was to gain the Abracadantès, there was another angle that so far remained oblique to me.

In sisterly fashion, Andi added, "Even if you do have all the puzzle pieces, you're not putting them in the right order."

"Speaking of things not being in the right order, I have to ask a favor."

"Of course."

"If anything should happen to me, will you take Ambrose for your apprentice?"

Andi's hazel eyes widened with alarm. "What do you think is going to happen to you?"

"Nothing. I'm just taking precautions. Ambrose likes you. His...family situation is complicated, but nothing you can't handle."

Andi only looked more worried. "You're going to talk to your aunt Iolanthe, aren't you?"

"I have to. If only to clear her of suspicion in my own mind."

"I don't like this. I *really* don't like this."

"You just told me you're sure Aunt I had nothing to do with Maman's predicament."

Andi stared at me, then sighed. "I did, didn't I? And I do believe that. So, yes. If something happens to you—and nothing better *had*   I promise to take Ambrose as my apprentice."

"Thank you. And—again, this is just a precaution—if something happens to me and Maman does not return, will you protect Jinx?"

Andi's jaw dropped. "Protect Jinx from *what*?"

"I'm not sure. Maman thought part of why she was summoned before *le Conseil Savant* was her decision to…take Jinx under her wing. If she's right, then it's possible the Société might pose some threat to Jinx."

Andi closed her mouth. She considered in silence. Finally, she said, "Jinx hates me. She's not going to accept my protection."

"Jinx is jealous of you. That's not the same thing."

"It's *close* to the same thing. Also, John is never in a million years going to let me tutor Jinx in the Craft."

"Jinx is her own person, but that's not what I'm asking. I know that would go against your own beliefs. I just want you to keep an eye out for her. She's kind of between two worlds, and there isn't anyone who understands what that's like better than you."

Andi glanced instinctively at the vintage Valentine pinned over her desk.

Valentine, you BEWITCH me!

They hadn't even known each other long enough celebrate an actual Valentine's day together, but there it was. He had even chosen something witch-themed.

She gave me a long, silent look. She nodded. "Not subtle, but okay. I promise, if necessary, to act as Jinx's fairy godmother." She sighed. "Anybody else you want me to take under my wing?"

"Well, Pyewacket might n—"

Andi rose—and so did her voice. "Oh no. No you don't. That's it! Cosmo, you darn well better get home safely or *else*!"

Chapter Sixteen

My aunt Iolanthe was not at home.

I had been so busy bracing for a possible confrontation, I hadn't seriously considered the fact that she might not be at her Fremont Street high-rise.

"She's in Paris," my uncle Lucien informed me, leading me into a room that seemed to be all windows, French oak hardwood floors, and views of the tops of other skyscrapers.

My uncle Lucien is not actually my uncle. Aunt I never married him, never took him as her beloved consort, but he is definitely more than her companion, and I've known him since I was thirteen, so he has always been Uncle Lucien to me.

"Paris? Why?" I accepted a tiny sherry glass brimming with ominously green liquid. Absinthe. I'm not a fan of absinthe, but Uncle Lucien is, and he views all visitors as an excuse to crack open the "green fairy."

"She's petitioning the Crone. Although Estelle specifically instructed her not to do so." He shrugged. "Iolanthe always thinks she knows best."

"Do you know what's really going on?"

Lucien is very handsome, very amiable, but not necessarily the sharpest knife in the cutlery drawer.

He tossed back his absinthe, blinked, and said, "These damned fanatics think they can overthrow nearly five hundred years of peaceful succession."

Four hundred and fifty-two years, to be exact, and the succession to the *trône de sorcière* wasn't always peaceful, unless you consider murder peaceful in comparison to outright war. Of which, I guess, an argument could be made.

"Is Waite with her?"

"Is Waite with who?" Lucien inquired.

"Is Waite with Aunt I?"

"Waite? No. Why would he be? He hates Paris." Lucien shook his head. "Sometimes I think that boy is a changeling."

My cousin Waite is not a changeling. He's the offspring of my aunt and her late beloved consort Walter Whitby. Walter was mortal and died when Waite was a baby. You would think being half mortal would give Waite a more enlightened world view, but he's one of the most virulent anti-mortal witches I know. Anyway, Lucien was a close family friend, and perhaps it was not surprising—per Maman——that after the crossing of Walter, Aunt I turned to Lucien for comfort.

"Does Aunt I believe the Crone will intercede on Maman's behalf?"

"If she does, she's a bigger fool than I think. The Crone is in as much danger as anyone, if you ask me. Not that anyone does in this house."

"But then—"

"I told Iolanthe, get the Queen out of Paris and back to Domrémy. But you know those two girls. They always think they know best."

"Which two girls?"

"Iolanthe and your mother." He studied his empty sherry glass as though it presented an unsolvable—and regrettable——mathematical equation. "Concatenation Integrity, my arse. The de Darrieux woman is behind it all. You'll see. I told your mother to poison her years ago, but no one listens to me."

Concatenation Integrity? The unbroken—no, *unassailable*—line of succession is what he referred to. As confusing as this was, I began to see a glimmer of light.

"I know that Maman and Thérèse de Darrieux were rivals at one time."

"It's all your father's fault. He was betrothed to de Dar-rieux. She was a distant cousin of your maman, seventh in line for the throne, back then. Ninth now. You know, no real threat. But your mother decided she would have your father for her own."

"You're kidding."

I love my father, but the idea of him as a chick magnet was just…no. And Maman as a poacher of another woman's fiancé? No way. And not just because Maman was not a woman ruled by passion.

"Not at all. As you know, because of the line of succession, your mother declined to marry your father, and I don't think he could really quite forgive that. After Arabella was born, he took up with the de Darrieux creature again." Lucien sighed. "And after Arabella… Well, it was all over between them. I think your mother blamed him for that as well."

As well as the failure of their relationship? Or as well as someone else she blamed? I wasn't sure. I asked instead, "What did happen to Arabella?"

Lucien stared at me. "Don't you know?"

"No."

He cleared his throat nervously.

"What happened to her?"

"I always assumed you knew."

I said again, "No." Honestly, until now I had not really wanted to know.

"Well, I… She was a very gifted witch. Very gifted. And a voracious reader. But she was a child. She read things she should never have been allowed access to. Fairy tales and such nonsense. Stories concocted by mortals about witches turning themselves into ducks and hares and all manner of ridiculous things."

My mouth went dry. I had a terrible feeling I knew what was coming, and I suddenly understood my mother's fierce antipathy for mortal books, mortal movies, mortal TV programs...mortals.

Lucien glanced at me, cleared his throat, said awkwardly, "Arabella created a potion she thought would turn her into a star. But the potion contained hydrogen cyanide."

I had no idea what to say. I had known that something too painful for my mother to speak of must be truly dreadful, but this was beyond my imagination.

"Your mother always believed someone put that idea in the child's head."

"Do you think that's true?"

He didn't meet my eyes. "I wasn't there."

"But?"

"I think Thérèse de Darrieux is a poisonous woman. But did she actually poison your sister?" He moved his head in firm negation. "No. Do I believe she will try to poison the Société du Sortilège against your mother? Oh yes. Very much so."

Chapter Seventeen

I half expected to see GramMa floating outside Aunt I's seventy-story high-rise when I reached the street following my talk with Uncle Lucien, but the afternoon skies were empty of anything but clouds and other buildings.

I felt shaken and a little sick after everything I'd learned. I believed the threat to the Duchess—perhaps to all of us—was even greater than I imagined. More than anything, I wanted to talk to John. I knew he was not happy with me. I knew he would be busy—he was always busy. But just to hear his voice would be a comfort.

Cars whizzed past, pedestrians strode by while I pressed his cell phone number and waited. I was not supposed to bypass Pat unless it was an emergency, and this was not an emergency——unless it was emergency of emotions, and John would not be sympathetic to that idea. Still, I waited as his phone buzzed across town.

An exhaust-laced breeze gusted through the steel and concrete towers, kicking up dust and the odd scrap of paper.

John spoke suddenly, crisply in my ear. "What's up?"

My throat tightened. I had to squeeze out the words. "I know you're… I just wanted to hear your voice."

He snorted. "You don't have to try to manipulate me. I already told you I'm not going anywhere."

It was a slap, but perhaps a slap I should have seen coming. That solid core of cynicism ran deep in John.

"That's not why." I had to stop.

"We'll work it out tonight, Cosmo. I'm sorry, but I don't have time for this right now."

I got control of myself. After all, what had I expected? He had said we would speak that evening. He had a plan in place, and I knew from experience, he liked to stick to the plan.

"Yes, of course. I just…I might be a little late. But I'll be there."

I could feel his frown. He considered lateness a sign of disrespect. "I see. Then I guess I'll see you when I see you." He clicked off.

I stared at my phone until the screen went black.

One of the good things about public transportation is it gives you the luxury of time to think.

In theory, I could have made the jump to Black Cat Estate, but it was about fifty miles, and that would have required a lot of energy. It was certainly farther than I'd ever jumped before, and the last thing I needed was to confront Waite when I was tired and drained. Plus, I'd only been to the winery a couple of times, and I didn't have a clear picture of it. I didn't want to risk landing in some other vineyard and spend the evening stumbling through rows of grape vines.

Instead, I took the BART to Richmond, watching the city flash by, seeing the occasional ghost or witch or jack-o'-lantern window dressing sail past. By then it was after four, and the sunlight was fading, the sky turning a milky yellow-gray. As we left the city limits, there were more trees turning autumnal colors, and even the grassy hillsides looked tawny and golden.

I had figured out by then that I was wrong about Aunt Iolanthe. She was not involved in the attempt to depose the Duchess. If anything, she was trying to help her. But I was not wrong about Waite.

Waite Whitby, a.k.a. *Count Whitney,* was up to his ears in this plot. And it was a plot. A plot that had been in motion for some time. My marriage to John had not been the reason behind the decision to remove my mother from the line of succession, but I believed it had been the inciting incident.

However, Waite could not be acting on his own. Or at least, it was unlikely. Waite was not what one would call a self-starter. Oh, he was ruthless enough, ambitious enough, but he was not clever or devious or particularly patient. Waite's idea of how to get rid of me continued to be to drown me in the nearest body of water. And as for Maman? Well, he wouldn't dream of tackling her on his own. That I was sure of.

Therefore, Waite had a partner. But who?

Thérèse de Darrieux.

That was possible. They seemed to share a common goal. Or…no. They shared an *immediate* goal, which was to remove my mother from the line of succession. But after everything I'd heard from Lucien, it was hard to believe that Madame de Darrieux did not have her eye on the ultimate prize, the *trône de sorcière*. And if it came down to Waite versus Madame de Darrieux, my money was on Madame.

Besides, Waite's confederate had to be someone closer to home, right?

No one was mailing blackmail letters from overseas. Not with postal rates the way they were these days. Anyway, the idea of Madame de Darrieux licking stamps and cutting out I KNOW WHO YOU ARE AND I SAW WHAT YOU DID from magazine pages was ludicrous. Whoever was orchestrating this blackmail scheme, it was someone here in San Francisco, someone who knew how it all worked, someone connected to SPMMR but not SPMMR, someone way more practical and savvier than Waite. Someone not afraid to get their hands dirty.

And that person—that link between Waite and those members of Société du Sortilège maneuvering for a change in leadership—knew things that only

My phone rang, interrupting my thoughts.

I'm embarrassed to admit I hoped it was John, regretting his earlier harshness.

It was not John. It was a number I didn't recognize.

I answered cautiously, and a woman's voice said, "Cosmo?"

She had the faintest French accent, and my wariness increased.

"Speaking."

"I'm not sure if you remember me. I'm Leonie de Foix. Rex's friend."

"Yes, Leonie. I remember you very well." My initial relief gave way to fear. "Has something happened? Has their condition changed?" Rex was nonbinary, preferring *they/them*.

"Yes." Her voice shook with emotion. "Their condition *has* changed. Rex has regained consciousness!"

I closed my eyes. "Blessed be."

"Blessed be," Leonie agreed. "I was beginning to fear... But it's all right. They're awake."

"That's wonderful news."

"Yes. Medicus Abioye says that within a few days Rex will make a full recovery."

Such is the power of the Healing Circle. When it works.

"I'm so glad."

"I knew you would be. Rex wants to see you right away. In fact, you were the first person they asked for."

"Me?" Rex and I were close, though sadly not as close as we had once been. Too busy building our careers and finding our place in the world. I was touched, but surprised.

"Yes. They say it's very urgent. They must speak to you and only you."

"When?"

"As soon as possible."

My gaze traveled down the crowded aisle. "I'm on my way to Sonoma. Is it possible we could speak by phone?"

She hesitated. "They're sleeping now. Perhaps when they wake. Only..."

"Only?"

"They were insistent they had to speak to you privately and in person. I think the matter is a delicate one."

"I hope to—should be—home later tonight. I'm not sure what time. I could come by the hospital early tomorrow perhaps?"

"Yes, I suppose." She still sounded doubtful. "It's only that they were so insistent that you speak as soon as possible."

"That's going to be as soon as possible," I said regretfully.

"Yes. Your Grace…I hope you won't think I'm overstepping…"

My heart skipped a beat. I had thought she might be Abracadantès, but Rex was not, so I had not wanted to assume.

"It's just Cosmo."

"Yes, but it isn't *just Cosmo*," Leonie replied tartly. "And I think that might be the trouble. I believe Rex was injured while working a case that involves the Abracadantès. I'm not sure, I could be wrong, but I think Rex believes your life may be in danger."

I didn't quite know what to say to that. I had believed Rex was working a case that had to do with SPMMR's vendetta against the Craft as a whole. In fact, I had been all but convinced Ralph had played a role in Rex's hit-and-run, although that seemed more doubtful after our last conversation.

I said, "That's alarming."

"Yes, it is. I hope you'll take great care, and come to see Rex as soon as you can."

"I will. I appreciate the warning. Tell Rex when they wake, not to worry. I'll be there as soon as possible."

"I shall. Thank you, Cosmo."

My phone had signaled another incoming call while I'd been speaking to Leonie. I clicked over, and saw I had missed a call from John.

With a feeling of trepidation, I pressed Playback.

"Cos, that was unfair," John said abruptly. "I'm sorry. I know you weren't—I know you were sincere. I apologize.

We'll talk it out tonight, and I promise I'll listen to you. We'll figure a way out of this mess together. That's all." There was an about-to-click-off sound, and he suddenly added, "And I love you."

That quick, added *And I love you* made my eyes sting. I played the message twice. Then I signed a few words of a protection spell, put my head back, and slept.

It was a quarter to five, and the train was pulling into Richmond when I woke.

A brisk, no-nonsense wind blew through the station area, sending people scurrying with their collars turned up and jackets clutched tight. I wished I'd worn a heavier coat. Especially after it took almost forty minutes to hire a taxi to take me the measly thirty-eight miles to the vineyard.

Times like these made me wish I'd taken John up on his offer of driving lessons. I could have managed the entire trip in about one third the time. Then again, given my iffy relationship with technology, I'd probably drive off a cliff the first time I left the garage, so maybe I was better relying on public transportation, Craft, and John.

The drive through rolling benchlands and hidden valleys was quiet and scenic. By the time the taxi reached the estate, it was sunset, and it seemed as though the sky had tipped over to spill out all its reds and purples and even a ripple or two of sauvignon-gold.

I paid the driver and got out, studying the Tudor-style brick mansion through the surrounding maples and magnolias. Lights gleamed cheerily in a few windows, and a red Ferrari 488 that I did not recognize was parked in the driveway. The house had been built by my Aunt Iolanthe and Uncle Lucien, but Waite had taken possession a few years ago. Beneath the house was a three-thousand-bottle wine cellar. Behind the house were tennis courts, pool, pool house, and fruit orchard. Waite and his fiancée, Jadis, did a lot of entertaining here, but they did not appear to be entertaining that Tuesday night, which was good news.

As I started up the tree-lined drive, my cell phone rang, and I reached into my pocket to silence it. But the phone wasn't having any of that. It jumped into my hand, continuing to vibrate. I pulled it out, and Andi's worried face appeared on the dark screen.

"Cos, after you left, I discovered a bad omen in a batch of raspberry-lemon cupcakes."

"What bad omen?"

"A baby raven's feather."

My stomach did an unhappy somersault. "Ugh. That's disgusting. How would a———"

Andi's tiny face squeaked, "Cosmo, *listen* to me!"

"I'm listening!"

"I had a bad feeling and decided to do some research on Madame de Darrieux."

The scrape of my boot heels on the brick drive sounded very loud in the twilight hush. I lowered my voice. "What did you find out?"

"Nothing."

A little anticlimactic, I must say. "Is that good news or bad news?"

"I saw a *photo* of her."

"Right. Well, I do know what she looks like, so—"

Andi wasn't wasting any time. She spoke right over me. "Remember when I said I saw Phelon having dinner at Gary Danko's?"

I said uneasily, "Yes."

"And you asked if he was alone? I said he wasn't, he was with a woman?"

"Yes," I said still more uneasily.

"That woman was Madame de Darrieux."

I stopped walking. "Are you sure?"

"Yes. Yes. A thousand times yes. I'm absolutely positive. She's got very distinctive eyebrows."

"Yes. She has those crazy-lady eyebrows."

"It was definitely her, and it was definitely him. And they were definitely as cozy as could be."

I stared through the low-hanging branches at the house. The wrought-iron lanterns positioned along the front glowed in cheery welcome. The tall chimneys and rooftop threw jagged shadows across the drive.

"Cos?" Andi prompted.

"I'm thinking."

At the very least, it was a lesson in the danger of preconceived notions.

The Black Mercedes that had struck Rex? Maman owned a Black Mercedes, and Phelon had had access to it all the time they lived together. Maman knew everyone in San Francisco high society, which meant Phelon knew everyone in San Francisco high society. In fact, Phelon wouldn't need Maman to provide an introduction to society. Plenty of people fawned over Eurotrash *royalty*. Phelon certainly knew Waite. They were even somewhat friendly. And all those things I had told Maman in confidence—things about John's heritage, things about our marriage, things that no one else knew? Phelon could have overheard any or all of those discussions. If he was willing to destroy the Duchess, he was certainly willing to listen in on her private conversations.

I had never once considered Phelon as a suspect.

And that had been worse than arrogant because if anyone should have known that Maman did not suffer fools and that Phelon could not possibly be the inbred dolt he seemed, it was me. I had allowed myself to be deceived by appearances and my own bias.

Andi said again, more urgently, "Cos?"

"I'm still here."

"Yes, you are," someone said from behind me.

I turned quickly, though not quickly enough, and something hard and shiny swung at me out of the darkness.

The flat side of a shovel slammed against my head.

I dropped my phone, which was squeaking in alarm, and pitched forward.

Just before everything went black, Phelon added, "But not for long."

Chapter Eighteen

"**Y**ou could have waited till we heard what he had to say."

I winced. Waite's voice hurts my head even when I don't have concussion.

"We know what he was going to say," Phelon answered. He added, in a light, affected tone that I guess was supposed to be me, "The Goddess won't like that! You're in trouble now!"

Waite muttered, "The Goddess *won't* like it."

"The Goddess is a myth just like their Jesus or any of the rest of it."

Waite's reply was too low for me to make out the words.

To which Phelon answered, "But you haven't come up with a better idea."

I unstuck my eyelids, pried open my eyes. I was lying on the floor. No, a marble hearth in front of a fireplace, and the bright yellow and red flames hurt to look at. I moved cautiously. My hands were bound. Tightly. My ankles were bound. Tightly. With rope, yes, but also with spellcraft.

"I didn't say I didn't want to kill him. I *want* to kill him. I'm saying, we can't do it *here*. He came by taxi. How are we going to hide that?"

"A forgetting spell." Phelon sounded his usual blasé and slightly bored self.

"On which taxi driver? We can't put a spell on all of them."

"What does it matter? So what if he came here by taxi? How is anyone going to prove that he didn't leave of his own free will?"

"On foot?"

"Why not? Anyway, they can't check with every single cab company and every single Uber or Lyft driver."

Oh yes they could. They could and they would. I had personal experience of that. They, whoever *they* might turn out to be in this jurisdiction, would check the trains too, and the buses, and truckers regularly driving this route, and random passing cars that might have picked up a lone hitchhiker.

"By the Lord and Lady, Phelon, *he's married to a police commissioner.*"

"Of a different city, in a different county."

"You really think that matters? You really think they won't search this place from top to bottom?"

"They won't find anything. Who cares?"

Far from calming my cousin, Phelon's easy-breezy what's-a-little-murder-between-family attitude seemed to be making Waite more agitated and nervous. "It isn't just about the police. We'll have reporters here asking questions. TV crews taking pictures. It's the last thing we can afford."

"No. The last thing we can afford is this little prick blabbing his mouth to anyone."

Waite fell silent.

I eased back a fraction, trying to see if I could get some leverage so I could push myself up. A large portrait of my mother hung over the fireplace. She gazed skeptically down at me. Except, it wasn't my mother. It was Aunt Iolanthe.

"What *do* you suppose his plan was?" Waite wondered from somewhere overhead.

I closed my eyes.

Phelon's voice joined Waite's. "I told you. Don't you watch any television at all? He was coming to tell you that he knew what you were up to, and if you didn't stop it, he would have to turn you in." He sounded amused.

"What? No. That's not—he had to have a better plan than that."

"It's true. It's what mortals do. I've seen it on *Poirot* many times. Also *Dateline*."

Maman would not approve of all that watching of mortal TV. Granted, Maman would not approve of any of this.

"He's not mortal."

"He might as well be."

My head was thumping in sickening time with my heart.

Would Andi go straight to John? I thought she would.

Was that good news or bad news? Did I prefer John in a fury to being murdered? I would have to consider... The floor squeaked as they moved away. I heard the *clink* of crystal, the splash of liquid. I closed my eyes, tried to focus.

> *These ties that bind must fall away*
> *I must be free to fight this day*

Nothing.

> *The bond of blood has proven false...*

Ugh. I really must have concussion if I believed there was suddenly a rhyme for *false*.

As though reading my thoughts, Waite said, "The Merriweather girl knows too much."

"Worse luck for her."

My heart skipped a beat. I renewed my efforts.

> *Hemp or cotton, rag or bone*
> *Release me now from danger known*

Again nothing.

Not even a twitch of the rope around my hands.

Neither Waite nor Phelon were truly adept, but they weren't using kiddie Craft either. I needed to pull myself together.

Goddess give me strength. Goddess give me courage. Goddess give me opportunity.

"If we could make it look like an accident…" Waite said slowly.

"Well, of course. What did you think I meant?"

"That we would bury him in Jadis's new rose garden."

Phelon chuckled. "It did cross my mind. The trenches are already dug. But you're right. If he disappears, it raises questions. If he has an accident, then it's a matter of proving it wasn't an accident, and that's not so easy to do."

I felt someone's gaze upon me. I turned my head and met the unblinking burgundy gaze of a ferret. Jadis's Familiar. Raphael, I think. Something like that.

I'm trying, I told him.

Try harder.

They say ferrets are loyal, affectionate, and smart, but give me a cat Familiar any day.

"Jadis can't ever know about this. No one can ever know about this."

Raphael and I exchanged looks.

Waite and Phelon really were very stupid. It would be beyond embarrassing to be killed by them.

"I wasn't thinking of putting it in my memoirs," Phelon drawled. "Anyway, no one is going to give a damn about Cosmo Aurelius Saville with Estelle out of the way."

"You really do hate her, don't you?" Waite said almost wonderingly.

Phelon made a *bah!* sound, which, frankly, was pure Maman. "I don't waste my energy on the woman. She must live with her choices like anyone else."

"Right, well so long as Mama isn't dr—"

"When I think of all I did for her! And she treated me like…like her plaything. *Me!*"

"Sure. I get that. This is just…politics."

"I was willing to make *her* my beloved consort. *Ha!* That I would have shared the *trône de sorcière* with that—"

"Yeah, I don't know that Thérèse would go for——"

This was interesting. I had assumed Waite had his eye on the throne, but clearly, he and Phelon had already worked out some deal wherein Waite relinquished his supposed claim in return for…what? Riches and power?

Waite was already rich. And power is very time-consuming. Like it or not, with power comes huge responsibility and one hell of a lot of bother. Both of which Waite is severely allergic to.

Meanwhile…

"*Thérèse!*" Phelon exclaimed. "She's another one. I do all the work, and she—"

From the other room, a phone rang, loud and shrill, cutting Phelon off mid-rant.

Between each slow, portentous trill of the phone fell a deep and deadly silence.

"It's done," Phelon said. His voice was flat.

My heart stopped.

What was done? What had these lunatics done? Was Maman dead? Was the Crone dead? Had the *trône de sorcière* fallen to these traitors?

Waite said nothing.

Footsteps retreated from the room. Waite muttered, "Fucking politics." I heard the whisper of leather, the squeak of the frame as he dropped down on the sofa.

Phelon's voice floated from the other room. "*Oui? C'est moi. Avons-nous remporté la victoire?*"

"You did this to yourself, Cosmo," Waite said.

I rolled onto my side. "How do you figure that?"

Waite scowled. His eyes were blue, his teeth straighter than mine, his chin dimpled, but, yes, we could have been brothers. We were not brothers, though, and had never felt anything close to brotherly love for each other. I had always believed that was because the *trône de sorcière* lay between us. But it seemed that was wrong. The differences were deeper and more fundamental.

"You don't even *want* the throne," he said bitterly.

"Apparently neither do you," I said. "*And* you're half mortal. Why would you be part of this?"

"Just shut up. It's already gone too far. There isn't any turning back now."

"Of course there is!" I struggled to sit up. "*Think.* So far you haven't done anything a good lawyer like Pierre Sjoberg can't get you out of. You haven't killed anyone yet. There's been one accidental death, one suicide, and a whole lot of extortion, which most victims will never admit even happened. But murder? Murder will destroy you in both realms."

Waite's mouth twisted. "As you constantly point out, there is only one realm."

"And, if you kill me, you'll be doing life without parole in it."

"I don't think so. I think Phelon is right. They would have to prove it wasn't an accident."

"Do you really think John is going to accept that I met accidental death here?"

He gave a stranger-things-have-happened spread of his hands, but really stranger things had *not* happened. No way would John accept my accidental death. And I couldn't help feeling that if John didn't get justice through the courts, he would find his own justice.

I opened my mouth, but the silence emanating from the kitchen suddenly sank in on both of us.

Waite half turned on the sofa. "Phelon?"

No reply.

"*Phelon?*"

Phelon appeared in the living room doorway. He looked ghostly white and stricken.

Waite jumped up. "What is it? What happened?"

"We've…failed."

Blessed be. Blessed be.

I closed my eyes in relief. Opened them.

"What?" Waite looked aghast. "*How?* That's impossible. You said it was a fait accompli."

Phelon's haggard eyes turned to me. "He had letters. *Thérèse* has been taken into custody."

"*He* had letters? What letters?"

"Not *him*. Estelle's—his father. He had letters written by Thérèse years ago. He kept them. Kept them all these years. Why would he do that?"

Insurance policy, I thought. I said nothing.

"What letters?" Waite demanded again.

"Letters she wrote him. She wanted him to be her beloved consort. She trusted him."

"But…"

I said, "I'm guessing Madame de Darrieux has wanted to assume the *trône de sorcière* since she was a very young witch. That she wrote of love and marriage and sedition."

Phelon's gaze burned into mine. "And betrayer that he is, he kept every word of them."

"*He's* the betrayer?"

But really, I didn't have time to waste on this. If Phelon had wanted me dead before, he wanted me all the more dead now. And Waite—Waite was too stupid, too venal to recognize where his best interests lay.

Raphael the ferret suddenly appeared on the fireplace mantle, squeaking loudly, which gained the attention of both Waite and Phelon.

Nothing else had worked so far. In desperation, I reached all the way back to childhood memories and Samantha

Spell-casting. I tried twitching my nose—and was so surprised when the ropes binding my feet slid off, I was afraid to move. In any case, the ropes around my wrists were still tight. I tried twitching my nose again, but no. The ropes remained fastened. Waite must have tied my ankles, and Phelon, my wrists. Phelon was probably the stronger of the two when it came to Craft. When it came to anything.

I had only seconds to decide. There were two of them and one of me. My chances of escaping with my hands still tied, were slim. But would I get a better chance than this? This might be it.

I did not believe I could talk my way out of this.

Even if Andi had immediately phoned John—and I thought she would—it would still take him time to get here. Even if John had immediately phoned local law enforcement— and I thought he maybe wouldn't—it would take them time to get here.

No. It was now or never.

I crossed my left leg, bent my right knee, rolled up and forward onto my feet. Not actual witchcraft, but with my hands tied behind me, it felt close.

"*Watch him,*" Phelon warned, and then, "Get him!"

Waite hurled his brandy glass at me. I ducked, and it smashed harmlessly against the stone fireplace.

Phelon went left, Waite went right, and it was clear they intended to outflank me. I continued to work to free my hands, but there was no play in the rope. I snapped my fingers, but nothing happened, so there was probably a holding spell upon me as well.

I twitched my nose at the squat brass lamp on the nearest table and sent it flying at Waite's head. I directed the coffee table at Phelon's knees. Neither connected with their target, but their being forced to jump out of the way gave me enough space to run for the doorway.

The round woven carpet flew out from under my feet, and I fell to one knee but managed to regain my feet. I dove through the doorway and nodded my head to pitch the heavy mahogany secretary desk against the wall, sideways.

I heard one of them crash into the secretary, but I didn't try to look back.

I gasped, *"Open a door in thin air, open a door that's always there—"*

A shining line of blue rectangle appeared—and pinched out.

So, yes, a holding spell.

I didn't slow, didn't falter. I kept running toward the front door, and I called out, *"Ticktock, turn the lock!"*

The rustic red front door flew open—and I flew out.

Someone came after me in an airborne tackle, locked arms around my waist, and we both tumbled down the brick steps to the cement drive.

I landed with the wind knocked out of me, and the next few seconds were a fight to haul breath into my lungs. Spots danced before my eyes. There was a ringing in my ears.

From overhead and behind the ringing, Phelon said, "Drag him to the pool. We'll drown him."

Waite, his knee still jammed in the small of my back, called, "Where the fuck are you going?"

"To my car. I'll be right back."

"Okay, get up," Waite panted. He pushed off me, and I rolled over and kicked him in the place I thought would do the most good—and the most harm. He howled, doubled over, and I tried to scramble to my feet. But I was a lot more tired now. Adrenaline and fear can only take you so far. I put my shoulder to the brick retaining wall, trying to lever myself up. At last, I got to my feet.

Out of the corner of my eye, I saw Waite straighten. His face was twisted and ugly with rage. He jerked his knee back and delivered a roundhouse kick with all his strength. It caught me in the hip, knocking me over the retaining wall into the hedge.

That hurt a lot, and though I did my best to kick Waite a few more times, sweat and tears blurred my vision and there was not enough strength left in my legs to do much more than leave bruises. The smell of damp earth and dead leaves filled my lungs.

Nox, luna argentea
De potestate mea fortitudinem tuam, excidetur
Diva, tuam miserere luceat

"Shut the hell *up*," Waite shouted. He slapped me so hard, my head snapped back, and as I tried to shake the reverberations out of my ears, dragged me out of the greenery.

I fought him every step of the way, but it was like punching through water. There was less and less force in my blows, and Waite didn't bother fighting back; he simply hauled me along, one hand locked in my hair, the other in my collar.

My hands scraped on the cement. The knees of my jeans ripped. I quit punching and began to grab for anything I could hold on to. Hedges, brick, grass, gravel…

We rounded the side of the house. I had a blurred impression of shining lamplight, damp-sparkled grass, a row of lounge chairs, and a pool twice the size of the one at home. It gleamed in the moonlight like a long blue tomb.

Footsteps came running from the other side of the house.

"What took you so long?" Waite's breath hung in the crisp autumn night.

Phelon sounded winded. "False alarm. I thought someone was coming up the drive, but they were only turning around."

"But where the hell did you *go*?" Waite demanded. "This asshole nearly ended my bloodline."

Phelon answered with an eerie lightness, "I thought we might need this."

There was a beat of silence.

"Where in the Nine Gates of Hell did you get that?"

At Waite's tone, I opened my eyes and saw Phelon holding a wand carved of ivory and jade. My heart froze. I had not been brimming with hope before, but I knew now I was all out of luck.

Phelon twirled the wand, said casually, "Supposedly it belonged to the Marquise de Montespan."

"You stole that from Auntie Estelle?"

Phelon laughed. "*Auntie Estelle?* Yes. I still have a key to Auntie Estelle's house. She didn't even think I was worth changing the locks for."

Waite couldn't seem to tear his gaze from the wand. The lamplight from the house behind us flashed and flickered off the jewels. "That can't be her real wand."

"Estelle thinks it is."

Waite swallowed. "Even if it is, you can't use another witch's wand. Especially *that* witch."

"It's bad form, sure, but of course you can." Phelon looked down at me and laughed again. "Oh my. Someone's having a bad night." He looked at Waite. "Go get a pair of swim trunks. I'll get his clothes off."

"Why?"

"Why do you think? Because no one goes swimming in their clothes. We'll put him in a pair of your swim trunks, turn on the fire pit, empty out a few bottles of wine, and it will look like the three of us were hanging out here drinking and swimming."

"He can't swim."

"Exactly. He fell in and drowned. That kind of thing happens all the time."

Only an idiot would believe that scenario. How did they plan to explain all our cuts and bruises? But Waite nodded, turned toward the house, and Phelon stooped down to drag me closer to the pool's edge.

I began to fight again, but I knew it was a losing battle.

On the edge of my vision, I saw Waite stop in his tracks. He was not having a change of heart, however.

He said in a very strange voice, "What in the name of the Goddess is *that*?"

Phelon instinctively turned—as did I——to gaze at the white mist slowly taking shape before our eyes.

Waite whispered, "Is that…"

"Of course not!" Phelon said fiercely.

And he was right. It was not the Goddess. Not even close. Ambrose's *grand-mère* floated in the night air, between our little tableau and the house.

"Waah dis evil?" she asked.

Phelon and Waite exchanged looks. Past their initial shock, they seemed more confused than alarmed.

"Is she a ghost?" It wasn't so much a question as Phelon thinking aloud.

Waite looked at me. "Is she?"

"No."

"Who is she?" Phelon asked.

I shook my head.

"You must have brought her with the wand," Waite told Phelon. His tone was accusing.

"That's not the Marquise de Montespan."

"How do you know?"

"I've seen paintings."

GramMa drew closer, sniffing the air. The night smelled of chlorine and woodsmoke and wet grass, but her wizened face grew tighter and angrier.

"There dark powa here," she whispered.

My scalp prickled. For once she was right. "Don't antagonize her," I warned them.

Phelon threw me a look of disbelief and laughed. "Are you serious? Are we supposed to be afraid of a vagrant crone who drifted in on the night wind?"

"Me a guh end dis now." GramMa raised her hands and, to my horror, began to cast her spell.

Four separate things happened then, though in my mind, they blended into one endless moment.

John silently rounded the side of the house, running in a half-crouch, with a gun held low.

Waite raised his hands and also began to spellcast.

Evil crone of unknown breed
End your spell or—

GramMa completed her spell and sent a bolt of green that sliced through Waite like a lance.

Phelon raised the Marquise de Montespan's wand, pointed it at GramMa, and cried, "*End eam nunc.*"

"No!" I shouted.

The tip of the Marquise de Montespan's wand glowed blue, and instantly, GramMa was encased in an unearthly blue halo.

I don't think she noticed. I don't think she even noticed that Waite had crumpled to the cement. She had already started a new spell, her whisper taking on volume and strength as her fingertips flickered green, then red, then green.

The blue glow around her seemed to darken and sparkle, and the entire cloudy mass exploded in thousands of glittering stars that died out before they touched the ground.

The sky was empty of all but a trace of blue smoke.

I had never seen Craft used to kill before. Now I had seen it twice in as many minutes.

John brought his weapon up. "Don't move," he said in a voice I had never heard before.

Phelon didn't even hesitate. He turned the wand toward me.

"*Conte—*"

I swept my legs forward, trying to knock Phelon over, which I managed to do. But as Phelon pitched forward, he grabbed for me, and we both tumbled into the pool. Before the water closed over my head, I heard John fire. I opened my eyes and saw red smoke twisting through the bubbles streaming past.

Phelon was screaming. I could hear his muffled shrieks, feel the wash and push of water as he flailed beside me.

We had plunged into the deep end. When my feet did not touch bottom, I felt a rush of pure panic.

Don't breathe in.

Don't breathe in.

Remember...

*"**N**ot being able to swim is a vulnerability, but a greater vulnerability is being this fearful."*

I rested my face in my hands, breathing in the smell of salt water and chlorine. "I know."

He pulled me over to him, so that my face rested in the curve of his neck and shoulder. He said against my ear, "I'm not going to let anything happen to you. I promise."

I nodded. I knew what he was saying—and what he wasn't saying. I drew away from him, turned my face. He gently squeezed the back of my neck, stroked my back, waiting.

As I stared at the blue and green squares of "moonbeam" tile, I suddenly noted a break in the pattern. Every few squares, there was a silvery blue tile with a five-point star design. I scooted away from John to peer more closely at the nearest silver tile.

Yes. It was a star...

I did not breathe in.

I hadn't had many swimming lessons. Our pool had only been completed a few short weeks before it grew too cold to swim. But John had insisted that I learn enough not to drown in our own backyard. I couldn't use my arms, but I could kick, which I began to do with all my strength.

Something hard and relentless sliced down through the artificially bright aqua, grabbed me by my collar, and hauled me up. Shoved me up and pushed me out. I landed on the cement, coughing and spluttering, chest heaving as I hauled in gulps of sweet night air.

"You're okay," John said. "You're okay now."

"N-not really."

He had already splashed back into the water. He was out in moment, dragging Phelon ungracefully onto the deck. I smelled blood and chlorine and something worse.

I remembered that as Phelon fell, he had dropped the wand into the water. I wriggled over, peered over the side, and I could see it lying at the bottom, winking and blinking beneath the still rippling water.

"Jesus fucking Christ Almighty..." John knelt beside Phelon, who was whimpering, facedown on the cement.

The whimpers turned into a scream as John used his belt to tie Phelon's arms behind his back.

John left him, checked Waite with a businesslike briefness that told me everything I needed to know, and scooted over to me. "You're okay, sweetheart. You're fine."

Well, not to complain, but I had been better. I had been knocked out. I had been beaten up. I had seen someone shot. I had seen two people die by magic. I had nearly drowned—*again.*

"That's it. Coughing's good. Clear your lungs." John helped me sit up, scanning my face. His own face changed, eyes going flat and black, mouth compressing, nostrils flaring. "No, you're not okay," he said thickly. His fingertips brushed my cheekbone, and I tried not to flinch. He gently pushed my hair back to see the cut over my eye.

I already had a scar there from the first time Waite had tried to kill me.

"Is Waite dead?"

"Yes." John pulled a knife out of his boot. "Lean forward."

I let myself fall against his chest, tried not to move, though I was shaking with stress and shock as he sliced through the ropes cutting into my wrists. I breathed him in, listening to the swift, efficient pound of his heart.

That would have been the worst part of dying. No more John.

"I don't think he suffered." John's tone was unemotional. He only cared because he knew I did. "I don't think either of them could have felt anything."

That answered one question. John had seen everything that happened. I had wondered if there had been time for him to register. I wondered what he made of it. He seemed unmoved. As though carnage was all in a day's work.

"Well, *I* feel something," Phelon cried. "You shot me. Remember? I'm shot."

We ignored him.

"Thank you," I said to John. "Thank you for coming to my rescue."

I tried to make it a joke, but it wasn't a joke, and he saw right through it. His arms locked around me. His voice sounded pained. "Of course I came for you. I'll always come for you. But why? Why did you do this? Why didn't you wait? I told you, we'd work it out together."

"Do you not notice I'm bleeding?" Phelon cried.

It looked—and sounded——like Phelon was not mortally injured. But he had already been falling when he had been hit. Which meant John had not planned to shoot him high in the shoulder. Which meant...

Which meant Phelon had nearly died trying to kill me.

Waite *had* died trying to kill me.

I wasn't sure I was ready to face that understanding.

"Because. Because it's not your job to clean up my mistakes," I told John. "I'm sorry I wasn't more careful. I will be from now on. I'll be discreet. I pr—"

"Hell yes, it's my job," John said impatiently. "It's my job to protect you. To love, cherish, and protect you. That's what I signed on for."

"But it's my job too," I said. "To love, cherish, and protect *you*. And I hate that I keep doing things that put you in the position of having to go against what you think is right just to keep my secrets safe. You don't even like secrets."

"You think *he* doesn't have secrets?" Phelon said with sudden poisonous softness.

John didn't even turn his head. "Your best chance of living through the night is letting me forget you're still here."

Phelon closed his eyes.

"Everybody has secrets," John told me quietly. "Yours are…a little more complicated than most. It doesn't matter how it started or where it ends. You're the one I love."

"Same. Always."

"You need to learn to trust me. We need to learn to trust each other." His face was stern, his eyes dark with emotion.

A turning point? Yes. For him and for me.

"Yes," I said. "You're right."

"Can you stand?" John asked.

I nodded, and he half lifted me to my feet, put his arm around me. I leaned into him.

"What do we do about…this? What do we do about Bergamasco?"

"Bergamasco is not a threat to you."

He said it with finality. So perhaps this was where the trust began. I would take his word that Bergamasco was not a threat.

"We need to call the local PD." John's mind was running in another direction. His tone was grim, anticipating the questions we could not answer, the publicity we could not afford.

I nodded. If it had been up to me… But it was not up to me, and so there was no way around it. I said apologetically, "It's going to be a long night." *Night* was being optimistic.

John didn't reply. He studied Phelon for a long moment. Phelon's eyes flashed to mine, and I saw a gleam of fear there.

I said, "In our silence lies our safety."

His lips parted. He closed his mouth.

I said, "We have to get that wand out of the swimming pool before the police arrive."

John nodded absently. "I'll use the strainer to scoop it up." He moved over to Waite's body. He rolled him over, and then looked up at me. "There's not a mark on him."

I shook my head. I didn't know what to say. I had never seen someone actually die. Let alone see someone killed by magic. That night I had seen two witches fall to the Craft. It had been a terrible sight. I knew it would forever change how I felt about many things, including my own power.

John continued to regard Waite's lifeless form. He said slowly, "I didn't realize the two of you looked so much alike."

"Yes. Maman and Aunt Iolanthe are identical twins."

"Yes, but it doesn't always…" He didn't finish the thought. He looked once more at Waite, looked at me, and his mouth curved into an odd, wolfish smile.

Epilogue

"**W**ait a minute," Bree said. "So, John's sergeant, the police, everyone, thinks *Waite* was the one who pushed Jinx's boyfriend out the window?"

I said, "He wasn't her boyfriend, and he didn't get pushed out a window. He fell off the fire escape."

"Uh-huh," Vaughn said, reaching over to top up Bree's coffee cup.

"Not funny," Andi told him.

Vaughn shrugged. "It's *kind* of funny. At the least, it's ironic."

I don't know what most Transformations of the Stag are like.

Mine was—belatedly—spent on Montara Mountain on Halloween night, four months after my wedding, talking and drinking cognac-laced coffee with the people I would have once said knew me best. The people who were still willing to give up their Samhain to wait with me beneath a golden-orange moon as big and ripe as a magical pumpkin. The five of us had not been together since the wedding rehearsal. The night Rex had been mown down in a hit-and-run. The night John had learned the truth of who and what I was. The night everything changed forever.

It seemed like a lifetime ago.

In some ways, it *was* a lifetime ago.

"And Phelon agreed to plead guilty to extortion and attempted murder and all the rest of it?" Bree's expression in the firelight was dubious, and I understood why.

"Yes."

"I wouldn't rely on that promise." Rex took a long swallow from their Thermos cup.

"No. I don't."

I did, however, rely on Phelon's fear of the Duchess—and of John.

Andi asked softly, "How's Ambrose doing?"

I lifted a shoulder. "Okay, I suppose. He's not talking much." Despite Maman and Bridget's combined efforts, Gram-Ma had been too powerful to contain. What she had recognized in me was, to her, a threat. I was afraid to contemplate how things might have ended had Phelon not interceded.

"Is he still working at Blue Moon?" Rex asked.

"Yes. He's working at the store, but he's taking a break from his training."

"Ah."

"That was nice of you and John to have him stay with you till he's back on his feet. Emotionally." Andi smiled at me. Despite the smile, I thought I saw sadness in her eyes, and I wondered if she had finally told Trace she couldn't marry him.

I said, "It was John's idea."

"Was it really?" Bree sounded amazed.

"Yes. It really was. He thinks Ambrose is a sharp kid and shows a lot of promise." I couldn't help a sigh. "I just hope he doesn't try to get him to join SFPD."

The others laughed.

In truth, I would be okay with whatever Ambrose chose for his path. He was struggling over the death of GramMa, feeling he should have tried harder, done more to protect her. Intellectually, he understood that a lifetime of spiritual anguish—the conflict between her innate gifts and her religious indoctrination—had driven her mad. But emotionally, he wanted something to blame, and that blame veered between himself and the Craft.

Vaughn said, "So you're saying John and Ambrose are at home tonight, handing out Halloween treats?"

"When I left, John was instructing Ambrose in the fine art of carving stencil designs onto pumpkins."

"You're kidding."

"Nope. They had already done a fox, a rabbit, and a tree."

"What do rabbits, foxes and trees have to do with Halloween?" Bree asked.

"Nothing that I know of."

John was just being kind. That, of course, did not fit any of their notions about John, but he was really good with Ambrose. Patient. Kind. But then John knew all about difficult family members. Which was why Nola also would be at the Greenwich house that evening, supervising the handing out of said treats.

As though reading my mind, Rex said, "You've got John's sister and Ambrose both staying with you?"

"Just until Maman gets home."

Which could not be too soon for me. John was way better with Ambrose than he was with Jinx. Jinx was partying with friends that night, to John's not-much-concealed disapproval—which was where he and I disagreed. I couldn't see any reason why Jinx shouldn't spend the night with friends. Or away from Nola.

"Oops. Full house," Vaughn said. "No more newlywed noogie for you two."

"It's *nookie*," Bree said.

"No, it's not."

"Yes, it is."

"Cos, is it nookie or noogie?"

Rex said, "It depends on the relationship."

We grinned at each other.

Rex was thinner and their hair was longer and wilder than ever, but otherwise, you would never know that they had spent the last months in what amounted to suspended animation while their body healed.

Andi pulled the neck fastening of her parka closer, and said, "I can't get over the fact that your parents are spending this entire week together in Paris."

"I'm sure Father is just staying at Maman's for the sake of convenience."

Rex cleared their throat.

Andi said, "Yes. That must be it."

"And I'm sure they have a lot to talk about after the—the blowup at *le Conseil Savant*."

I had yet to hear the details of what had occurred at the last convening of the *Société du Sortilège*. I knew—everyone in the Abracadantès knew——that the membership of *le Conseil Savant* had changed yet again. Madame de Darrieux had reportedly been banished. In the Craft we call it *burned*. It is the harshest of punishments, at least in modern times.

Oliver had gone into hiding—again—but I did not know if he had been officially sanctioned. For that matter, I was not really clear what his role in the attempted coup had been. That he was rabidly anti-mortal was now clear. I was sure, though I had no proof, he had been working with Phelon. Yet he was ostensibly friends with Ralph and, as far as I could tell, had been aiding and abetting SPMMR.

I did know, after meeting Ralph for drinks that week, that the Society for Prevention of Magic in the Mortal Realm was satisfied with the outcome. Which right there was enough to make me uneasy.

Bree said, "I think it's kind of romantic that your father kept those letters all those years in case the Duchess ever needed them."

Vaughn turned to give her a look of disbelief. "You think it's romantic that Cosmo's father kept letters to be used as blackmail if necessary?"

"Well, yes. Sort of."

"This is why I text," he said.

Andi and Rex laughed.

We threw more wood on our little fire, drank more coffee, then dispensed with the coffee and just drank cognac. The moon drifted slowly across the sky.

Vaughn and Bree eventually zipped their sleeping bags together and curled up for the night.

"And we always said it wouldn't last," I remarked soulfully.

"*Shut up, Cosmo,*" Bree's muffled voice returned, and then she squealed and started giggling. I heard Vaughn's deeper laugh join hers.

Andi and I smiled at each other. Rex topped off our cups and shook the last drops out of the thermos.

The three of us chatted a while longer, and then Andi sighed, said wistfully, "That's it, then. Life is back to normal."

Her eyes met mine, and I felt a pang.

Yes, she had told him, and her heart was breaking. Trace's too, I didn't doubt.

"It seems so," I said.

After Andi had rolled herself into a neat little jellyroll of sleeping bag, Rex and I talked about what had happened the night Phelon had tried to kill Rex.

"Did you know there was a plan to remove Maman and make Madame de Darrieux heiress to the *trône de sorcière*?"

Rex made a pained sound. "No. I knew Phelon was working with SPMMR and had been for some time. I thought—wrongly—that the plan was to either frame you for murder or kill you outright. I didn't realize it was *une affaire de malice domestique.*"

I let out a long sigh. "Yes. So it seems."

Rex poked the fire absently.

I said slowly, "Phelon was being helped by members of SPMMR. I don't care what Ralph says."

"Ralph may not know," Rex pointed out. "SPMMR is a growing organization. Just as there are factions within the Craft, factions within the Abracadantès, factions within your own family, so there are factions within SPMMR."

"True."

I studied them for a moment, smiled. "This reminds me of the night we spent in the Schwarzwald."

Rex smiled in return. "Yes. Those were good times."

"We never did make it to Aokigahara Forest."

"No."

For a time the only sound was the pop and snap of firewood.

Rex said in a low voice, "Are you happy, Cosmo?"

I didn't have to think about it. "Oh yes. Very."

Soulmates is not a thing within the Craft, but I did believe that in John, I had found my soulmate.

Rex regarded me in that steady way, and seemed satisfied. "I'm glad."

A thought occurred to me. "Is your case closed?"

"No." Rex amended, "One angle of investigation has closed."

"Does your ongoing investigation concern me?"

Rex shook their head. "No."

That was a relief.

By then it was very late and the moon had slid behind the tawny hillside. The only light was our fire. The shadow flames seemed to link hands and dance through the trees...

Rex yawned abruptly and rose. "I'll say good night, then."

I gazed up at Rex. "Good night. Thank you for being here."

"I wouldn't have missed it."

Our eyes met, our mouths curved, knowing how nearly they had.

Rex unzipped their bag, climbed inside, zipped it up. "You have to keep the fire burning, you know."

"I know."

Rex settled their head on their bundled jacket, and closed their eyes.

It became a struggle not to fall asleep.

The night grew colder, darker, eerie, but each time I thought of John waiting at home for me, I felt warm and happy and calm. The old doubts were gone. I didn't know what the future held, but I knew we would face it together, and that was the only promise I needed.

More time passed.

Somewhere to the east, an owl hooted. I listened and wondered. Witch's lost Familiar, or a wild creature?

I whispered, *"We must each find our place in the world."*

The fire continued to crackle and sing. Embers drifted into the sky.

"For each of us there is a place in this world."

The air changed.

I gazed into the heart of the fire. As I watched the flames jump higher and higher, I saw it begin to take form, saw a stag with hooves of fire and horns of flame, saw the stag grow in long licking leaps of yellow and red tongues.

I rose and spoke the final words. *"Show me my place within this world."*

My heart pounded in time with the swirling, molten heart of the stag.

I was afraid, and I was full of joy.

So mote it be.

I opened my arms.

Author Notes

I know what you're going to say. I promised you a trilogy, and now I'm announcing *Bell, Book, and Scandal* is the final book in the first arc of a six-book series. So yes, my intention is to write three more books of a more stand-alone nature: *Hex in the City, Bump in the Night*, and *Impractical Magic*. As much as I love the first three books in this series, I was originally planning on something a bit lighter and funnier. But writing, like any other magic, has a way of unfolding in ways that are not always predictable. We'll see what happens next time.

If you are new to this series, yes, the police procedure is largely based on television shows of the 1970s (yes, I KNOW that San Francisco police commissioners operate as a commission and are not omnipotent) and true, there is no actual Witchcraft tradition known as Abracadantès.

Whether burning a witch or writing a book, it takes a village. So thank you once again to the incomparable Keren Reed for working her magic. Thank you to the Office Elf. Thank you to our newest bright spirit, R.R., for casting her spell upon these pages. Thank you to the SO (or as he's known around the castle: Graphic Designer, Master Chef, Dog Distractor, Guardian of the Gate, and I'LL-GET-THAT). Thank you to Kale Williams for—among other things—being willing to tackle Latin in a French accent. Thank you to my patrons for keeping the cauldron boiling and the home fires burning. And finally, thank YOU, dear readers, for buying this book. If you enjoyed it, please consider leaving a review.

About the Author

Author of over ninety titles of classic Male/Male fiction featuring twisty mystery, kickass adventure, and unapologetic man-on-man romance, JOSH LANYON's work has been translated into twelve languages. Her FBI thriller *Fair Game* was the first Male/Male title to be published by Harlequin Mondadori, then the largest romance publisher in Italy. *Stranger on the Shore* (Harper Collins Italia) was the first M/M title to be published in print. In 2016 *Fatal Shadows* placed #5 in Japan's annual Boy Love novel list (the first and only title by a foreign author to place on the list). The Adrien English series was awarded the All Time Favorite Couple by the Goodreads M/M Romance Group. In 2019, *Fatal Shadows* became the first LGBTQ mobile game created by Moments: Choose Your Story.

She is an Eppie Award winner, a four-time Lambda Literary Award finalist (twice for Gay Mystery), an Edgar nominee, and the first ever recipient of the Goodreads All Time Favorite M/M Author award.

Josh is married and lives in Southern California.

Find other Josh Lanyon titles at www.joshlanyon.com, and follow Josh on Twitter, Facebook, Goodreads, Instagram and Tumblr.

Also by Josh Lanyon

NOVELS

The ADRIEN ENGLISH Mysteries

Fatal Shadows • A Dangerous Thing • The Hell You Say
Death of a Pirate King • The Dark Tide
So This is Christmas • Stranger Things Have Happened

The HOLMES & MORIARITY Mysteries

Somebody Killed His Editor • All She Wrote
The Boy with the Painful Tattoo • In Other Words...Murder

The ALL'S FAIR Series

Fair Game • Fair Play • Fair Chance

The ART OF MURDER Series

The Mermaid Murders •The Monet Murders
The Magician Murders • The Monuments Men Murders

The SECRETS AND SCRABBLE Series

Murder at Pirate's Cove • Secret at Skull House
Mystery at the Masquerade • Scandal at the Salty Dog
Body at Buccaneer's Bay

OTHER NOVELS

The Ghost Wore Yellow Socks
Mexican Heat (with Laura Baumbach)
Strange Fortune • Come Unto These Yellow Sands
This Rough Magic • Stranger on the Shore • Winter Kill
Murder in Pastel • Jefferson Blythe, Esquire
The Curse of the Blue Scarab • Murder Takes the High Road
Séance on a Summer's Night • The Ghost Had an Early Check-Out

NOVELLAS

The DANGEROUS GROUND Series
Dangerous Ground • Old Poison • Blood Heat
Dead Run • Kick Start • Blind Side

The I SPY Series
I Spy Something Bloody • I Spy Something Wicked
I Spy Something Christmas

The IN A DARK WOOD Series
In a Dark Wood • The Parting Glass

The DARK HORSE Series
The Dark Horse • The White Knight

The DOYLE & SPAIN Series
Snowball in Hell

The XOXO FILES Series
Mummie Dearest

OTHER NOVELLAS

Cards on the Table • The Dark Farewell •The Darkling Thrush
The Dickens with Love • Don't Look Back • A Ghost of a Chance
Lovers and Other Strangers • Out of the Blue
A Vintage Affair • Lone Star (in Men Under the Mistletoe)
Green Glass Beads (in Irregulars) • Blood Red Butterfly
Haunted Heart Winter • Everything I Know • Baby, It's Cold
A Case of Christmas • Murder Between the Pages • Slay Ride

SHORT STORIES

*A Limited Engagement • The French Have a Word for It
In Sunshine or In Shadow • Until We Meet Once More
Icecapade (in His for the Holidays) • Perfect Day
Heart Trouble • In Plain Sight • Wedding Favors
Wizard's Moon • Fade to Black • Night Watch
Plenty of Fish • The Boy Next Door
Halloween is Murder*

COLLECTIONS

*Stories (Vol. 1) • Sweet Spot (the Petit Morts)
Merry Christmas, Darling (Holiday Codas)
Christmas Waltz (Holiday Codas 2)
I Spy...Three Novellas
Point Blank (Five Dangerous Ground Novellas)
Dark Horse, White Knight (Two Novellas)
The Adrien English Mysteries
The Adrien English Mysteries 2*